CITY OF SNARES

CITY OF SNARES

by April Yates

Edited by Elle Turpitt

Formatted by Stephanie Ellis

Cover illustration and design by Daniella Batsheva

First Edition: November 2023

ISBN (paperback): 978-1-957537-87-0

ISBN (ebook): 978-1-957537-86-3

Library of Congress Control Number: 2023948746

BRIGIDS GATE PRESS
Bucyrus, Kansas

www.brigidsgatepress.com

Printed in the United States of America

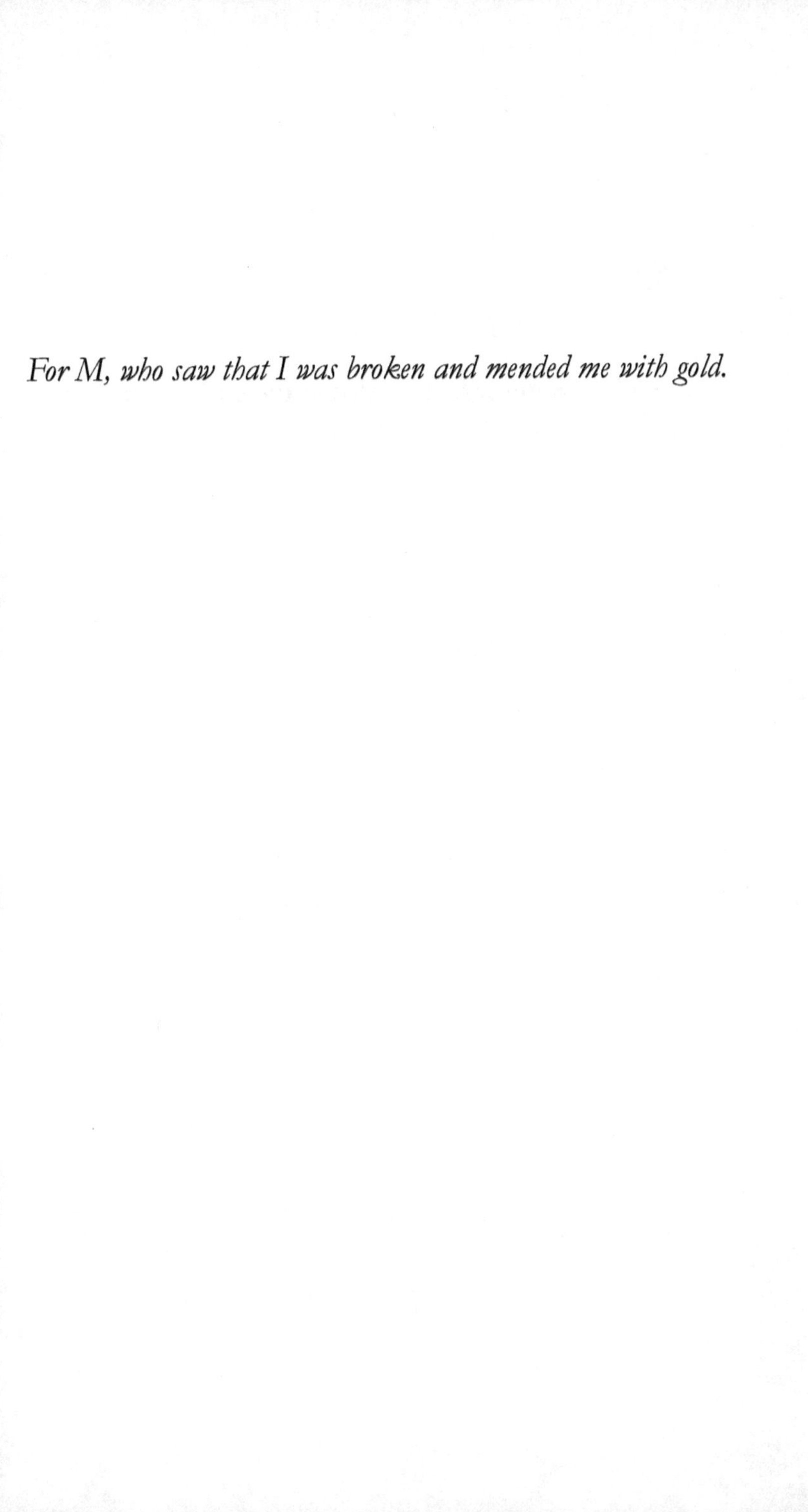

For M, who saw that I was broken and mended me with gold.

Content warnings are provided at the end of this book

CHAPTER ONE

Truddi Tuttler's Tinseltown

BOX OFFICE POISON!

Harry Brandt's red boarded ad in the Hollywood Reporter last month has sent shockwaves through Tinseltown with Garbo, Crawford and Hepburn careers already taking a swan dive into the sewer (though some would argue they were already there).

Now with word on the lot that Diana Blake's newest picture has been placed indefinitely on the back burner it seems that there is no antidote available to counteract Brandt's poisonous words …

***

"Fuck off," this from the drunk in the corner. He didn't seem to be talking to anyone in particular. His arms sprawled in front of him and head resting on the table, a small puddle of spittle pooled beneath his mouth.

None of this had registered with Hazel, because sat at a table was Diana Blake and she was even more captivating in the flesh than Hazel could ever have imagined.

Every sound of the diner seemed muted as if passing through water; the gentle sizzle of oil on the grill, the burbling of the coffee pot, even the drunk in the corner booth's muttered ramblings had taken on that faraway quality.

"Are you going to stand there all night or are you going to see what the broad wants?" Louie, the fry cook, asked Hazel, not unkindly. It was three in the morning and by the disinterest Louie was showing he could not have recognised Diana.

True, she wore minimal makeup and her normally elegantly coiffed hair was loose, reaching to her shoulders. Still, Hazel would've recognised that face anywhere, had spent her life transfixed by it ever since she was five years old and her father had taken her to the Picture House cinema in her hometown, a town five thousand miles and a lifetime away now.

As Hazel walked over, for the first time ever she was painfully aware of the wrinkles in her uniform shirt. She held her notepad in front of her apron, attempting to hide the coffee stains. She'd served other stars of the silver screen, but never had she felt as nervous.

Granted, none had been Diana Blake's calibre.

"What can I get for you, Miss Blake?" Hazel said, feeling rather proud of how casual she sounded.

Diana took a drag of her cigarette, her eyes narrowed and fixed upon Hazel. Heat rose on the back of her neck, as if she had committed some terrible faux pas.

Was Diana attempting to be incognito, and she'd ruined it by announcing her name to the, admittedly empty, diner?

Finally, Diana said, "You're new here."

"I've been working here for three months, going on—"

She held up her hand, cutting Hazel off. "I didn't mean …" Diana paused for a beat before making a sweeping gesture with her hands, the glowing end of her cigarette moving perilously close to Hazel's bare arms. "Here. I meant America, this town."

"I came over just five months ago, from—" Hazel began.

"You have no family here?" Diana talked over her, eyes locked upon Hazel's as she did.

"Yes, no family."

Diana couldn't possibly be genuinely interested, Hazel thought, but could think of no other possible reason why she'd be asking these questions.

"How old are you?"

"Twenty-two."

Diana's gaze left Hazel's eyes, fixating on a point behind her.

Should I leave, give her more time to think? Hazel thought, *Evidently she's lost interest in me.*

"I want a coffee. Black, and when you bring it to me you are going to sit down and talk to me."

"That's really very kind of you, but I don't think I ought to whilst I'm working."

Diana looked around. The drunk in the end booth gave a soft snore whilst Louie, engrossed in one of the many pulp westerns he kept behind the counter, wouldn't have noticed if a grease fire started.

"I'm sure you taking a five-minute break won't make the whole joint descend into chaos."

"No, I suppose it won't."

She walked back to the counter and poured Diana's coffee; Louie didn't even glance up from his book. Hazel debated whether to pour a second cup for herself. Too presumptuous?

Hazel returned to Diana's table, placing a solitary cup in front of her before sitting down.

"So," Diana said, lighting another cigarette, the tip of which, Hazel noticed, was red rather than the usual cork. "I can see from your tag that your name is Hazel and you obviously know who I am so we needn't bother with formal introductions." She pushed the coffee cup towards Hazel. "Drink that, you look dead on your feet and I need you to pay attention to every word. I can think of only one reason a pretty young thing would travel all the way from …?" She stopped here and Hazel could only assume that she was waiting for her to fill in the blank.

"Edenton."

Diana looked blank.

"It's a little village in England, Der—"

"And that's to be a star, be on the arm of one, or both."

"I could think of a dozen or so other reasons," Hazel said rather waspishly. It irked her to be thought of as being so shallow, so vapid.

"I'm sure you could." Diana smiled for the first time, putting Hazel at ease. "Tell me truthfully now, Hazel. Do you want to be in pictures?"

"Yes." Was that the truth? Her thought was interrupted by more of the drunk's incoherent ramblings. "Bloody Nora, what's he blarting about?" Hazel muttered.

"What kind of talk is that?"

"It's—"

"It's unrefined is what it is. Marks you as low class but," Diana took a deep drag, "we can fix that. I want you to meet me tomorrow night at Florentine Gardens. Do you need the dollar fifty to get in?"

Hazel nodded yes. She made thirty cents an hour at the diner, and on nights like these tips were hardly forthcoming.

"That won't be a problem. Normally I wouldn't be caught dead there, such a tawdry place, but for you I'll make an exception. It's a shame I had to see you here first, but we'll fix it."

"I don't understand."

"Lana Turner may have been spotted drinking a malt at a drugstore counter, but that's not going to work for you. It makes for a much better story for Francis to discover you there rather than here. Florentine Gardens is perfect. It has that shallow glamour but is still accessible to Jane Doe dreaming of being a star."

Diana flicked her cigarette end into the still full cup before standing and casting that apprising gaze upon her again.

"Yes, I think you'll do very well. I'll be there around nine. Don't worry about finding me, I'll find you. Here." Diana produced a ten-dollar bill and, stepping close enough to Hazel so she could feel her breath on her neck, tucked the note into her breast pocket.

"Yes," Diana whispered. "This will do very nicely."

Then she was gone.

Had you asked her after, Hazel would not have been able to tell you how long she spent staring at the door waiting to see if Diana would return. But she would have told you it was until the drunk in the corner started shouting for coffee.

CHAPTER TWO

The ten-dollar bill clasped tightly in her hand, Hazel stood in the ladieswear section of Sears debating the individual merits of, to Hazel's eyes at least, the near identical dresses in front of her.

Since coming to America she had only worn a skirt to work, the rest of the time, without her mother's nagging, she'd been free to wear slacks. The wearing of which still managed to elicit mild looks of derision from those above a certain age. The looks were worth it though; they were more comfortable as well as practical.

Hazel wasn't naïve enough to think she could get away with wearing them out to Florentine Gardens.

Should I even go at all?

Hazel had come to Los Angeles, casually flirting with the idea of fame and fortune, facing the possibility of it coming true induced a sense of nauseous excitement. She'd spent every spare penny, every spare moment sat in darkness staring at that picture screen wishing she could be there away from that place, away from her family.

But going to that club? Was it wise? Who was Francis? Her roommate Quinn had told her stories of the casting couch.

The thought of sleeping with any man, let alone to do so to gain an advantage, made Hazel's stomach clench.

I should walk away now. I could put that ten dollars to good use, save it for an emergency.

Instead she bought a blue woollen dress for four dollars, the most she'd ever spent on clothing.

****

"Where did you get the cash for that?" Quinn asked, as Hazel held the dress up to herself in the mirror, desperately trying to imagine what she'd look like in it. "Yesterday you couldn't afford to pick up milk." Quinn drew closer to her, eyes narrowing. "I've never seen you in a dress before. What are you up to?"

Hazel decided some half-truths would be best. "My family sent me some money and I've had an invitation to go out to Florentine Gardens," she said so quickly she very nearly tumbled over the words.

"A man?" Quinn asked.

"Yes, he came into the diner, asked if I'd like to have dinner with him. I really would like to look my best. Would you help me? Please."

Hazel wondered if Quinn would notice how fast she'd spoken, but Quinn ploughed on regardless.

"I thought I'd never see the day that you would be fussing over a man. I was starting to think you were like my Aunt Pauletta."

"Excuse me?"

"Never married, lives with a lady friend. But we all know what that means. Mother hasn't spoken to her for years."

Hazel bit the inside of her cheek, a habit she'd developed years ago whenever she needed to remain unreadable.

Quinn carried on. "Daddy would never have her in the house, even if her and Mama had still been talking of course, goes against nature." She paused, taking one of Hazel's hands in hers. "I'm happy for you." She squeezed Hazel's hand before letting go and continuing with her spiel. "You must tell me all about him, of course. What does he do? Is he from a good family?" Quinn picked up the dress. "You chose a good colour, it goes well with your complexion." She held it back up in front of Hazel.

Quinn was right, Hazel thought as she looked in the mirror again; her skin steadfastly refused to tan, even the California sun only brought a light smattering of freckles. But the cool blue of the dress suited her ash-blonde hair and grey eyes, making them pop.

"What time?" Quinn asked.

"Eight." *Five more hours,* Hazel thought, *and I'll be in her presence once again.*

"Oodles of time. I'll do your hair and makeup, you'll look like a movie star."

***

Eight o'clock and Hazel stood outside The Florentine Gardens; the night air was cool but the sweat trickled down her neck.

The Gardens were built in the style of a Moorish palace and, even before she went in, Hazel found herself agreeing with Diana's assessment of the place being cheap and tawdry. She paid the cover charge and inside found a spectacle of half-naked showgirls clattering plates and musicians. Hazel wished she'd asked Quinn to come with her. She felt like a lone lamb surrounded by potential wolves. Seated in a dark corner, a waitress took her drink order.

She sat and drank alone, ignored by all.

She left at ten, alone, ignored by all.

After the heat of the club, the night was blessedly cold. It had rained whilst she was inside, the street gleamed and shone red, white, and green, a carpet of jewels across Hollywood Boulevard.

Across the street a car sat, its engine idling. A woman at the wheel lit a cigarette. In the glow, Diana's face. She smiled at Hazel before driving away.

Chapter Three

It had surprised Quinn to see her home so early. When Hazel told Quinn she had been left alone, Quinn called the imaginary man a scoundrel, and a bastard. Told Hazel she could do better.

It pushed them from two women sharing an apartment to something approaching friendship.

***

"I'm mashin', want one?"

Quinn turned to face Hazel from where she was applying her lipstick in the mirror by the door "I don't think I'll ever understand how you can 'mash' tea. It just makes it sound thoroughly unpleasant."

"Pardon me." Hazel put on her best impression of an upper class English lady. "I'm about to brew a pot of tea. Would you care for one?"

A smile tugged at the corner of Quinn's lips. "No time, I'll be late for work." She went back to checking her appearance in the mirror a moment. "Hey, would you like to go see a picture tonight?"

"Um …" Quinn had never invited her anywhere before.

"You're not working tonight, are you?"

"No, I'm working the lunch shift."

"So?"

"That'll be great. I'd love to go."

"Fantastic, I'll see you tonight," she said as she left.

Hazel turned to clear the breakfast dishes but was interrupted by a knock on the door.

"Forgotten something," she called as she crossed the room.

"Delivery for Hazel," a young, male voice said from behind the door. She slid the chain on before opening the door a fraction. A delivery boy stood there with the biggest bouquet Hazel had ever seen in her life, a beaming smile on his face.

She closed the door, slid the chain off, and opened the door fully.

He passed her the flowers, put his hand to his cap and said, "Have a nice day, ma'am," before hurrying off.

Nested amongst the blooms was a card upon which, in spidery flowing letters, was written, *I should have come inside.*

***

Quinn had chosen a Diana Blake picture.

"I loved her movies as a kid," Quinn said as they sat down.

"Yeah, me too."

She thought of the flowers set on the table at home. She'd removed the card; though there was no name, the hand was decidedly feminine.

Hazel couldn't focus on the story as Diana loomed large on the screen.

She knew she was even more beautiful in the flesh.

She had smelt her perfume.

Felt her breath on her neck.

Had in her pocket that promise of something more.
I should have come inside.

***

It had been over a week since Hazel had been stood up at the Gardens by Diana when, approaching the end of her night shift, Hazel saw Diana's car parked outside the diner.

The time went by slowly as Hazel waited for the clock to turn six; shift over, she rushed outside.

The car door swung open. "Get in."

Hazel obeyed.

Diana started the car, a smug smile on her lips as they drove in silence. It was light when the car turned onto Sunset and it was only then Hazel asked where it was they were going.

"My house," Diana said.

Hazel's eyes were stinging. She closed them, and focused on the sound of Diana's breathing, so soft and so close.

As the time passed, Hazel's mind wandered back to that night, to how foolish she felt, waiting alone whilst Diana was outside. The dull roar of blood rushing replaced all other sounds as her chest began to pound. She'd heard nothing from her since the flowers. They'd already died, much like the hope they'd inspired.

Suddenly the car stopped moving. Hazel opened her eyes to find Diana watching her intently, with a cold, clinical look that sent Hazel's anger to the forefront.

"You left me waiting for you like an idiot. Why didn't you come inside?"

"I wanted to know for sure you would follow instructions. You looked beautiful, in fact quite stunning, by the way."

She is not telling me that she finds me beautiful, merely that I possess these qualities for others to see.

Still, Hazel felt a stab of satisfaction.

"Come inside and see the house," Diana said, getting out of the car.

Diana's home was French Revival, all crooked rooflines and non-linear window arrangements. All designed to evoke the sense of the place rather than adhering to any kind of historical accuracy. It was like something out of a storybook, with ivy clinging to the turrets and second story overhangs.

Diana led her inside, their shoes clattering on the tiled floor.

"Perfect for dancing," she told Hazel.

They left the foyer and went through to the kitchen, where Diana sat Hazel down at the breakfast bar and told her to wait. The room was nearly as big as Hazel and Quinn's entire apartment, and decorated in pale pink polka dots, broken by blue-and-white polka dots.

The scent of lemon disinfectant assaulted Hazel's nostrils, the same brand that she and Quinn had bought on occasion for their apartment, though unlike her home there wasn't an underpinning of rot.

Diana returned holding a red bathrobe.

"Put this on. What would you like to eat? I have eggs and bacon." She was already getting the items out of the refrigerator and heating a frying pan.

"Bacon and eggs would be lovely," Hazel replied, but thought, *there's only ever an illusion of choice with this woman. Everything is already decided.*

Diana placed the bacon into the hot pan. The sizzle was loud in the cavernous kitchen and soon the air was smoky and fragrant. Hazel's empty stomach gurgled.

"Get that dirty uniform off, it makes me uncomfortable. I don't want grease stains everywhere."

Hazel picked up the robe and turned towards the door.

"You can do that here."

Once again, Hazel felt compelled to obey.

As Hazel undressed, Diana put bread into the electric toaster and cracked two eggs into the pan alongside the bacon. All the time whilst she worked, her eyes remained on Hazel, but for the brief glances she afforded to her tasks.

Once she was down to her underclothes, Hazel reached for the robe.

"No, take it all off, it needs washing."

Hazel looked at Diana with a look of mild indignation, which was no match for Diana's withering stare. Relenting, she dropped the robe onto the counter.

Hazel turned her back to Diana to finish undressing, not thinking that she'd have to turn around to get the robe from the counter anyway.

Feeling bold, she faced Diana, taking her time and letting her take in all of her before putting the robe on. She cinched the belt tight and bent to pick up her clothes.

"Where should I—"

"Leave them there. They'll be taken care of."

Diana set the plate down in front of her. "I reckon it must be a long time since anyone fixed you a home cooked meal." She moved around the counter until she stood at the back of Hazel, her fingertips grazing the back of Hazel's neck as she started to remove her hairpins. "I'm guessing that even when you were at home with your mom you weren't truly looked after or doted on."

All the pins removed, her fingers teased the tangles out. Hazel shivered and was sure she heard a mocking laugh in response.

***

Once Hazel finished eating, Diana beckoned her once again to follow. The bedroom she led her to contained the biggest bed Hazel had ever seen, adorned with pale blue sheets and more pillows than could ever be necessary. There were two plush armchairs in that same shade of blue and a pine dressing table complete with a mirror edged with bright white bulbs. Through an open door, Hazel could see an en suite.

Could I actually be in Diana Blake's bedroom?

Diana gestured toward the bed. Hazel didn't need to be told twice, she let the robe fall to the floor before sitting down on the edge of the bed, nerve endings alight with expectation.

Diana moved towards her and, placing her palm on Hazel's chest, pushed her gently back onto the bed. Hazel scrambled backwards until she was fully on to allow room. Diana turned away and closed the door behind her.

Leaving Hazel alone in the semidarkness.

***

The sunlight was streaming through the window when Hazel awoke; it felt like mid-afternoon but she couldn't be sure; there were no clocks visible in the room.

She made her way to the bathroom, her head heavy with the remnants of sleep.

All the fixtures were blue, matching the soft furnishings in the bedroom, the floor and walls were such a glossy white Hazel had to squint against them. She ran the tap, filling the sink with cool water. After splashing her face, she felt more awake and began to assess her situation.

Why had Diana brought me here? Undressed me?

It struck her, the reality of how vulnerable she was, Diana had taken everything. She had no clothes, no money, hell, she didn't even know for certain where she was.

Feeling dizzy, Hazel sat down on the toilet. From this new vantage point, Hazel saw the rim of red circling the base of the sink. It was the thinnest of lines, but against the gleaming white title, it may as well have been an inch thick.

She dropped to the floor, the cold ceramic painfully hard on her knees, but she needed to look. Hazel dipped her nail into the minute gap. The red stuff was tacky. Then she saw it. Behind the back of the sink base was a tooth. Hazel stared, morbidly fascinated by its long and bloody root.

"That woman, I told her a dozen times that this room was to have a guest. She's getting old. The eyes and mind have a tendency to go." Diana leaned against the door frame, cigarette in hand. "Get off the floor, it's obviously dirty." She pitched her spent cigarette onto the tile. "Elsbeth, clean this up."

No sooner had she given the command, a woman armed with a mop and bucket came rushing in. Elsbeth looked as if she had broken seventy whilst the five-foot mark remained firmly intact.

"We'll leave her to it."

***

It was pure naivety to believe that the room Hazel had slept in was Diana's own. Hazel had thought that room was opulent, but it was nothing compared to the room she was in now.

17

The room was a soft pink dominated by a wrought iron four-poster bed above which was a mirrored ceiling. Hazel blushed at the thought of Diana beneath it, her beneath Diana. She looked away from the bed, thankful that Diana had disappeared into the walk-in wardrobe and couldn't see the state in which she had got herself, again.

As Hazel lingered by her dressing table examining the crystal perfume bottles, she noticed a diamond-encrusted watch worth twenty years of working at the diner, casually tossed amongst the jars of cold cream and witch hazel oil bottles. A fleeting thought of *that could set me up for life* was quickly suppressed. It would be obvious who had taken it and Diana knew far too much about her. She'd be in a cell before she made it to the nearest pawnshop.

"Here." Diana held out a pair of black slacks and a white sweater.

"Why was there a tooth in the bathroom?" Hazel asked, trying to keep her tone one of mild disinterest.

Diana tossed the clothing onto her bed. "You know how it is, darling, you have a few friends over, everyone gets liquored up, someone falls flat on their face. You felt how hard those tiles are. I'm surprised he only lost the one."

"He?"

Diana laughed. "I'm not married, so I'm free to have a gentleman friend or two." Diana sat on the bed, Hazel's underclothes washed and pressed beside her. "You thought I was that way? I suppose never say never but it's something I've never thought to try. It doesn't bother me though, that you're a dyke."

"I'm not—"

"Because any adult woman who would strip down and jump into another woman's bed at a drop of a hat ..."

"It wasn't your bed," Hazel protested pathetically.

"You thought it was my bed. Wanted, needed it to be mine. I could smell the want on you."

Shame pulsated through her. How could she have thought even for a second that Diana would or even could ever be interested in her that way?

She'll never want to see me again.

Hazel feared she had taken acts of kindness and turned them into something sordid.

She's normal, how could she ever want you like THAT?

"There's plenty like you scattered amongst the studios, but if you want any kind of success, you need to keep it a secret."

"I'm hardly going to take out a newspaper advert," Hazel said, the words sticking in her throat like shards of glass.

"Get dressed, it's a beautiful afternoon to sit by the pool."

"Thank you, but I need to get home so I can get ready for work tonight."

"I sent a note explaining that you wouldn't be coming back, along with your uniform. Cleaned. Dried and pressed, of course."

"You have no right. I've got bills and rent to pay. I have to go, I'm going to have to beg them to take me back."

"For fuck's sake, would you stop with the hysterics? You have a meeting with Francis on Tuesday."

"Who the bloody hell is that?"

Diana strode over, undid the gown's belt and pushed it from Hazel's shoulders, the fabric pooling around her feet, and for the third time that day Hazel stood vulnerable and bare before her. This time, however, she could not hide. Her hands still firmly on Hazel, holding her in place, Diana leaned forward, placing a kiss on her forehead. The gesture was meant as chaste, motherly even, still it sent a shiver down Hazel's spine, shame quickly following.

"All will be well, I promise," Diana said, brushing Hazel's cheek gently with the back of her hand. "Now, be a good girl, get dressed and come downstairs."

CHAPTER FOUR

They spent hours by the pool in deep conversation. Diana wanted to know every detail of Hazel's life since coming to Los Angeles. They went over her arrival, her meeting, then moving in with Quinn.

Diana even questioned her about past lovers.

"Yes, I've been with someone since coming to America …"

"Yes, there were a few girls back in England …"

"No, I've never been with a man … Yes, I'm quite certain I wouldn't like it …"

"I remember when I first saw Bedevilled and you came out in that dress …" Hazel blushed. "Well, I thought you were the most gorgeous thing I ever saw."

Diana smiled, and there was genuine warmth in her eyes as she said, "Thank you." Then, "It was all downhill from there. The men—Hazel, a man becomes distinguished, not just in this business but all aspects of life. It's nature's cruellest trick …" Her voice cracked ever so slightly, the practised mid-Atlantic accent slipping. "Cherish it while you have it Hazel, it's all too fleeting."

How can she look in the mirror and not see what I see?

Not see that she was—is-perfection?

"Do you not want children?" Diana asked, pouring a measure of vodka into a highball glass before plucking three ice cubes from the silver bucket, ignoring the tongs. Her tone once again like cool silk.

"You've never had children," Hazel said. "Do you regret it?"

"People have children so that a part of them lives on after they're gone. Me? I'm going to live forever."

"Through your films?"

Diana laughed. "Of course. That's what I meant." She gulped down the reminder of her drink. "I'll drive you home."

***

Hazel was just about to put her key in the latch when Quinn flung the door open.

"Where have you been?" she hissed, pulling Hazel inside. Quinn looked Hazel up and down. "New clothes, again? Have you been with him? After he let you down again? Any fella who jerked me around like that would soon learn the hard way what happens—"

Hazel held a finger to her lips. "Please," she said. "Not now, my head is pounding." She pushed past Quinn to the small kitchenette. Sitting at the table she noted glumly how hard the chair was, how pitted and chipped the Formica table top was.

Has it always been this fucking depressing?

"And another thing," Quinn resumed her tirade. "Why are you not at work?"

"You don't have to worry about my share of things," Hazel said, laying her head on the table.

Why is my head so fuzzy? I didn't have that much to drink.
Then nothing.

***

Both the door and Hazel's head were pounding. She was in her own bed, but couldn't remember how she got there.

Did Quinn help me, or did I make it under my own steam? Quinn must've been out, as the knocking continued.

"Hold on," she shouted, pushing herself off the bed. Still fully dressed in Diana's clothes with shoes still on. Quinn didn't have to put her in nightwear, but taking her shoes off would have been nice.

She made it from the bedroom to the apartment door and, flinging it open, it did not surprise her to find Diana there.

"You shouldn't sleep in cashmere."

"I've bloody well had it with people telling me what I should and shouldn't do," Hazel muttered, moving aside to let her in.

Hazel looked around the apartment, seeing it through Diana's eyes, how must it look to her compared to her own home?

Nothing was dirty, but everything was shoddy. From the threadbare sofa to the peeling paint coming off the skirting in ever-increasing swaths.

Diana's nose wrinkled in distaste. "Charming," she said, rummaging amongst the contents of her purse.

The need to defend her home reared up within Hazel and she couldn't stop herself from saying, "It's not much, but maybe you've forgotten how normal people have to live."

"The farm I grew up on was not much more than a shack. It's been a long time since then, but I've never forgotten."

Hazel tried to recall a magazine article she had read long ago that said Diana was born in a city.

Detroit? Des Moines?

No mention of a rural setting as far as she could remember, but she could, well, must be confusing Diana with someone else.

"I swore that I'd do anything to get away. That's what drew me to you. I think you'll do anything too."

"Why have you come?"

"To prepare you for Tuesday, of course. You need an outfit, nothing too glamorous. We are cultivating an English rose persona here."

"We?"

"Yes, we. Together, we'll make your dreams come true. I'm going to take you for lunch, then shopping."

Why the intense interest? Was Diana so lonely as to latch on to her? But as what? A friend, mentor, substitute daughter? Although she didn't look it, Diana was old enough to be Hazel's mother. In fact, she was a few years older than her mother.

"After we've got you a few pretty things, I'll take you for drinks. Some place nice." She placed her hand on the small of Hazel's back. Hazel felt Diana's thumb moving, drawing small circles. Once again Hazel's body betrayed her. Diana smiled, fully aware of her effect.

"No need to change clothes, you'll do as you are. You can brush your hair in the car."

***

They spent the afternoon in stores Hazel could never have even dreamed of setting foot in by herself.

And, true to her word, Diana took her out to dinner afterwards.

Was this all, despite Diana's protests, a courtship? After all, she was treating Hazel as a man might treat his mistress. "I like this one," she had whispered to her as they stood before a mirror in the boutique. "It shows off your curves."

Hazel had gazed at herself in the mirror, emerald-green silk with black embroidered starbursts; it hugged her waist accentuating her figure, turning it into a near perfect hourglass.

Somehow she felt more exposed in this gown than she'd ever been in her life.

It had been bad enough when it had just been her, Diana, and the shopgirl. Now, sitting in Musso and Frank's backroom, she felt like an imposter.

Diana looked perfectly at home, though maybe a little over dressed for the warm weather, in her polar-white furs and elbow-length maroon gloves.

Diana reached into her bag and, taking out a small box, slid it across to Hazel.

"A gift."

Hazel opened it. Nestled inside was a silver bracelet adorned with emeralds and diamonds.

"To match your dress," Diana said. "Do you like it?"

"I love it!" She fumbled, trying to do the clasp with one hand for a moment before Diana, with a sigh, stubbed out her cigarette and leaned across the table and took the bracelet.

"Hold out your hand."

As she clasped the bracelet she whispered, "You've such delicate hands, I should think they're very talented." Diana slowly brushed her thumb over her wrist and Hazel's pulse leapt to meet it.

She smiled before letting Hazel's hand drop.

"Valentino used to come here," Diana said loudly, fishing the cherry out from her whiskey sour and passing it to Hazel to dispose of. "Garbo still does."

Hazel looked around. There were two dozen patrons in the dining room; some she recognised, most she didn't. To her horror, as she looked around Hazel accidentally locked eyes with a dark-haired man. She quickly broke away but it was too late. He excused himself to his companions and made a beeline to her and Diana.

"Diana, wonderful to see you." His eyes flicked down to Hazel's breasts. "And who is your charming little friend?"

"Francis, this is your appointment for tomorrow, Hazel."

Francis' mouth turned up into a wolfish grin. He extended one meaty paw towards Hazel, enclosing her hand. As he bent to press his lips to the back of Hazel's hand two things happened simultaneously. Hazel saw Francis' eyes widen in disgust, and she felt a sticky wetness between her fingers.

The cherry.

Francis withdrew his hand and stared at the smashed red jewel in his palm. Diana took a sip of her sour, smirking.

"I'm so sorry—" Hazel began, but before she could finish her apologies, he erupted into laughter.

"Classy broad. Where you find this one, Di?" Francis said, picking the remains of the fruit from his hand.

"That's for you to decide." Diana placed one maroon-gloved hand upon Hazel's upper arm . "She's yours to mould into a modern myth."

"You know, there's not a lot of women who'd be so keen on lining up their own box-office replacement."

"I believe in the next generation."

The way they were talking about her as if she wasn't there made her feel like a small child amongst adults.

"I'll see you tomorrow," he said. His eyes flitted once more to Hazel's chest before he went back to his own table.

"You certainly made an impression," Diana drawled. She finished her drink and motioned for another one by holding a finger up.

"I forgot I was holding it," Hazel whispered.

"Why were you even holding it?" she asked as she looked at the menu. "What do you want to eat?"

Out of pettiness, Hazel searched for the most expensive items on the menu whilst Diana gave her order to the waiter.

"I'll have the double tenderloin steak with béarnaise sauce and potatoes au gratin, and canapé of caviar to start, please," Hazel said, earning a look of amused derision from Diana. Her meal alone came to over four dollars. Her minor victory at thinking she'd upset Diana was short-lived as she once again fixed Hazel with that gaze.

"You've room for a few more inches around the hips, but don't make a habit of it."

"I think I might want a pudding afterwards as well."

Diana gifted her with a small laugh in response. "Point taken. So how do you feel about tomorrow?"

"Confused, who exactly is Francis?"

"He's the kind of man who can take a Spaniard and turn her into an all-American girl."

"He discovered Rita Hayworth." The squeak of Hazel's voice betrayed her excitement. It had been all over the magazines about the transformation of Margarita Carmen Cansino, Latin dancer, into Rita Hayworth, all-American actress, a process described in great detail including before and after photos.

"No, Henry Cohn, over at Columbia, was responsible for her, but the same basic idea."

"Is there something wrong with the way I am now?"

"That's for the studio to decide."

***

Diana insisted Hazel spent the night at her place once again, and once again she followed her to the bedroom.

"You know I'm perfectly capable of putting myself to bed."

"It soothes me to know that you're safe."

"Really?"

"Yes, and don't furrow your brow like that, you'll get wrinkles."

She went to the wardrobe and took out a nightgown.

"I had Elsbeth clean and press these for you." She indicated to the still open door. The wardrobe was full to bursting with clothes; evening and day, casual and formal, and everything in between.

"How, when?" Hazel managed to stammer.

"Today, once I knew your size, I had the shop girl pick out a selection, she knows my tastes."

Hazel knew she should've been mad, insulted that Diana saw her as a paper doll to pin her wishes and fancies up on. But her continued interest flattered her.

She ran her fingers along the stack of fabric; even the hangers were opulent, wrapped in plush satin, no cheap bare wire here.

"I'll look after you," Diana said, placing a kiss on Hazel's forehead.

Diana's lips were cool, but they caused a cascade of heat to tumble through Hazel.

"Why?" Hazel's voice was heavy, thick, and the word came out as little more than a sob.

Diana placed a firm hand on Hazel's jaw, forcing her to look up and meet her intense gaze, fevered blue eyes boring into her

"Because I can."

Chapter Five

Truddi Tuttler's Tinseltown

A CERTAIN member of the so called "Box Office Poison" list was once again seen stumbling out of the Cocoanut Grove with a beau on her arm young enough to be her son. Once one of the brightest stars in the TKO Studios stable, her light is fading and it won't be long before another shining light eclipses her entirely …

***

Voices drifted in from the hall, low wavering voices like waves lapping on the shore. It was still dark outside; the only light was a thin bar creeping beneath the door.

Hazel switched the lamp on the bedside table and squinted at the new wristwatch Diana had bought her. It was three-thirty in the morning. She got out of bed and tiptoed to the door. The low drone transformed into legible words.

"Keen, aren't ya?" The voice was male, drunk. "Whores like you never can wait."

Hazel's hand darted for the door handle, ready to defend Diana. Before she could open the door, Diana's crystal tones rang through.

"No, I can't wait, so why don't you get in that bed and show me what you've got? Or do I need to find a man who hasn't drunk himself into a state of flaccidity?"

Diana was stone cold sober. Despite the drinks she knocked back at Musso's, she was in complete control. Did she enjoy being spoken to this way? Hazel had known women like that. But Diana did not sound excited, she sounded like a woman undertaking a necessary but laborious chore.

Hazel opened the door a sliver, just enough to see that Diana was still wearing her gown from dinner. The man was a smouldering pillar of anger, swaying slightly as if caught in the gale of Diana's words. He staggered forward, grasping Diana's neck as they slammed into the wall. Diana laughed.

"So, you have some fire in you after all."

She pushed him away easily before leading him further down the hall and behind closed doors.

***

Hazel and Diana were in the dining room separated by a great swath of French-polished wood, the intimacy of the kitchen gone.

Hazel never saw the man leave. Unable to get back to sleep, Hazel had watched for hours, waiting for him to walk past her open door. She wanted to have a better look at this person who Diana had deemed good enough for her bed. After hours of waiting, Diana appeared at her door, impeccably groomed and coiffed, to tell her to get ready.

"You should have this," she'd said, placing the diamond watch from her dressing table in Hazel's hand.

"You've got so many opportunities coming your way, you're going to want to be on time."

Elsbeth set down a fresh pot of coffee between them before placing a silver ashtray by Diana.

"That'll be all, thank you, Elsbeth."

She waited until Elsbeth had left before pouring her coffee, adding a generous glut of milk and sugar. Hazel poured her own cup but as she reached for the milk pitcher Diana gave her a look of mild rebuke, which reminded Hazel of the look her own mother would give her as a child when she caught her trying to sneak an extra biscuit.

Hazel left the milk and took a sip of the thin, bitter liquid.

Diana took out her silver cigarette case and placed one of her rose-tipped cigarettes between rose-red lips, before sliding the case towards Hazel.

"No, thank you."

"You should start, a man loves to watch a woman smoke, it gets them riled up, makes them think what else you could be doing with your mouth, your lips, your tongue."

Hazel coughed, sending a spray of coffee across the table.

Diana laughed. "Works on you. It'll also help you maintain your weight."

"I'm fine, really." Even as she said the words, out of curiosity Hazel took one, it was pure decadence. The rose petal was supple and fragrant and Hazel could not help but imagine that Diana's lips must be as soft as that petal.

"Before the war, I'd have them shipped over by the case from England, when production stopped I didn't want to go and find a new brand so I dedicated a part of the garden to growing the same variety of rosebushes. Elsbeth cuts and glues them fresh each morning." She lit up before continuing. "This is what's at stake for you today. The power and resources to have anything you want, no matter how frivolous. You may think you have that right now, that you are a woman of independence, but you're not and until you've tasted it, Hazel, that absolute control, you can't comprehend it."

***

Francis's office reeked of the sickly sweet smell of his rum-and-maple cigarettes, the ashtray on his desk near overflowing. Hazel noticed that not all of them could be his though, unless he had a secret predilection for lipstick. The second thing she noticed was the movie camera looming, an almost malevolent presence to rival Francis himself.
"You're a looker. I'll give you that much." He leaned back in his chair, putting his feet up on his desk. "Why don't you give me a ..." He made a spinning motion with his forefinger.

Hazel turned slowly around, feeling his eyes taking in every inch of her.

"Very nice." He motioned for her to sit on the couch beneath a large window where the light streamed through. The sofa was a blue velvet fading into teal where the sun had bleached out the colour.

Hazel placed herself down in the centre. Despite the plush look of the cushions, it dipped, so the wooden battens dug into Hazel's thighs.

Francis moved from behind his desk to the camera. He stood beside the machine, running the back of his hand down its side in a caress.

"We'll see if the camera loves you as much as Diana does." He turned it on, a cacophony of clicks and whirls.

"What do you want me to do?" Hazel asked.

"Emote."

"Excuse me?"

"I'm going to list a variety of situations and you'll react accordingly. For example, your fella has just given you a bunch of flowers and a box of candy. How would you look?"

Hazel thought of all the times she'd been given a gift and coupled it with the wide-eyed melodrama of every picture she'd ever seen.

She felt idiotic, but Francis seemed to like what he saw.

"Good, good, now fear."

She pulled the appropriate facial expressions.

Smiling broadly.

Furrowing her brow.

Widening her eyes.

Each one eliciting another, "Good, good."

"I'd like to do something a little different now," he said, sitting down beside Hazel. "It goes without saying that you're not going to be on the soundstage by yourself. I need to know how you play with others." He shifted closer. "I know I'm not as handsome as some of the leading men we have on contract. But I think I have a certain charm."

Francis put his massive hand on her knee.

"Hazel, a beautiful girl like you will have to play romance. Look at me like you adore me. Want me." His grip on her knee tightened.

Is this normal behaviour?

Francis had a congenial smile on his face that said, *Hey relax, it's all pretend you know.*

She looked down at the chubby fingers, the tips of which were nicotine yellow, and revulsion leapt into her throat, threatening to spill out.

She swallowed the feeling back down, and when she looked back up, she was beaming.

"Good, good." He shifted even closer. 'Good' seemed to encompass the majority of Francis's vocabulary.

His hand slid up Hazel's thigh atop the fabric and for the first time in her life, she was glad to not be wearing trousers, so that his hand could not easily slip between her legs.

"Kiss me."

"No, thank you."

Francis laughed, but a hard glint remained in his eyes, betraying his fury. "Hazel, would Gone with the Wind have been a successful picture if Bret had given Scarlet a pat on the back and a handshake?" He removed his hand and stood up.

"I'm sorry, this is all new to me," Hazel said quickly, realising that her safest option was to assign all blame to herself. She was painfully aware of how close he was still standing. "Maybe I'm not leading lady material. I'm sorry to have wasted your time."

She tried to stand.

"Hey, where do you think you're going?" His voice a low growl. "Do you think this is all free, that I did this for nothing? You have any fucking idea how expensive this all is to set up?"

"I'm sorry, really—"

Hazel tried again to move off the sofa. He pushed the heel of his palm against her chest, forcing her back down, then went to his desk and lit a cigarette.

"I don't even know why I'm bothering with you," he said, taking a drag on the cigarette. Unlike Diana, who held it between her middle and index fingers, delicately brushing her full lips. Francis held his between thumb and index finger, puffing his cheeks up like a chipmunk as he held the smoke in his mouth. "Plenty of women willing to do what it takes to make it in this town."

He came back over, kneeling before her so his face was level with hers, and exhaled that sickly smoke in her face.

"So," he said, his hand going to her knee, under her skirt and travelling up her thigh. "Are we going to come to an agreement?"

Her breath hitched in her chest as his hand moved further up her thigh.

What can I do?

Her entire chest felt as though it had been put in a vice, each movement of his, a turn of the handle crushing it tighter.

You need to leave, now.

Hazel looked at the cigarette in his hand, its end a furious red.

She snatched it away, careful not to extinguish it with her own fingers, and pushed the glowing end into his cheekbone, eliciting a roar.

Both hands went instinctively to his face, making him lose his balance, and he fell to his side on the floor. Hazel scrambled over him, made it to the office door, unbolted the latch and then out into the safety of the hallway.

She pulled her skirt down, wiped away tears she hadn't even been aware of, and walked as calmly as she could down the hall.

***

Hazel stumbled outside onto the lot. After the dim hallways the sun was blinding in her tear-stained eyes. She walked until she found a telephone, desperate to reach someone she could trust.

Hazel dialled the party line number shared by the residents in her and Quinn's apartment building.

The engaged tone rung out, no doubt the woman down the hall. She seemed to be on that line morning, noon, and night.

Unable to reach Quinn, Hazel collapsed onto the floor, giant wrecking sobs cleaving her chest in two.

No money, except for a few nickels, and miles from home she had no choice, she had to find Diana.

She closed her eyes, breathing deeply.

Had Diana known what Francis would try? No, she wouldn't throw her to a wolf. Expect her to …

That was the whole point of Diana taking her under her wing: so that she'd be protected, shielded. Diana cared about her.

Diana cares.

Diana cares.

"What the fuck have you done?" Diana stood above her, sunglasses obscuring her expression, though her tone was unmistakable. "Get the fuck up."

She bent down and grabbed Hazel's upper arm, jerking her up with surprising ease.

She handled Hazel roughly, marching her around a corner where they were out of view.

Once alone, Diana produced a handkerchief and thrusted it at Hazel.

"Clean yourself up, you're a disgrace."

The initial shock had worn off and the anger that had been simmering within Hazel reached boiling point.

"It's you that made me come here. I was happy enough with my life until you started meddling with it."

This was greeted with a derisive snort by Diana.

"Why are you so bloody obsessed with me? I'd understand if you wanted me to fuck you, but you claim that isn't the case. I don't understand you. I know what Francis wants from me, but what do you have to gain, Diana?"

Diana looked around, the sounds of the lot surrounded them, but there was not one person in sight. They could have been anywhere.

The kiss she pulled Hazel into was dry and hard, devoid of passion, but spilling over with desperation. Hazel knew deep down that Diana was manipulating her, God help her though. That nagging thought of *what if?* was relentless. Diana stepped back, once again looking to see if anyone could see them.

"That answer your question?"

"No, it doesn't."

"I want what's best for you. You'd do well to trust me."

"Trust? How can I trust you? Did you know what Francis would try to do to me?"

"I didn't think you were so naïve, Hazel."

"No, I understand what goes on in this town. I just never imagined that you'd send me in like a lamb to the slaughter like that."

"I told him you wouldn't be desperate enough to sleep with him, that at the most you'd maybe blow him," she muttered.

"You really are something. Well, after what I did to him I think my screen career is a no start anyhow."

"What did you do?"

"I shoved the lit end of one of those God awful cigarettes into his face."

Diana smirked.

"It's not funny. I'm surprised I haven't been dragged off to a cell by now." Panic gripped Hazel. "Oh God, what if I get sent back to England?"

"Francis won't say anything."

"How can you be sure?"

She seized Hazel's jaw, forcing her to look up into her eyes, a gesture that was becoming increasingly familiar to her.

"Because I know. I'll not tell you again."

Chapter Six

Hazel insisted that Diana take her home, her real home.

"Fine. I'll take you to your dingy little apartment, shall I?" Diana slammed the car door.

"Yes, I'd like that very much," Hazel said petulantly.

They drove in silence from the studio until reaching Hazel's building. As Hazel opened the car door, Diana reached across, catching her wrist.

"You need to toughen up, Hazel," she said. "I'll give you a few days to sort yourself out."

Hazel opened her mouth in a retort, but it died on her lips.

***

"You've been with that man again, haven't you?" Quinn said as Hazel walked through the door.

Despite her tone, the look on Quinn's face was one of such utter sincerity and concern that the tears Hazel had been holding back spilled over.

"I'm sorry I shouted. I was just so worried about you." Quinn took Hazel in her arms. "It's okay, no man's worth all this. Especially when there's plenty of others out there who'll treat you right."

This elicited a fresh batch of tears; Hazel couldn't stand to lie to her any longer.

Hazel broke gently away from her and went to sit on the sofa.

"Quinn …" Hazel didn't know what to say next. Quinn sat down beside her, taking her hand gently.

"Did he hurt you?"

"Quinn, I need to tell you the truth. I'm not who you think I am. I never have been. There is no man in my life. Never will be."

"What do you mean?"

Hazel took a deep breath, preparing herself for Quinn's reaction. She might have to find somewhere else to live, and just when she and Quinn were getting along better than they'd ever done.

"I don't like men. Well, I like men. But just not in that way."

"So, it's a woman who's been treating you this way." Quinn fell silent, her brow slightly furrowed in thought. "Huh?" she said, eventually. "I guess I was right after all. You are like my aunt."

"It is a woman I've been seeing. It's Diana Blake."

Quinn looked at Hazel, eyebrows raised.

"But not in that way!" Hazel hurriedly added.

"Diana Blake. The actual Diana Blake?"

Hazel nodded. "I'm her little project. The next big thing she wants to mould me into."

"And this is not a good thing?"

"No, it's not. Diana arranged a meeting at the studio. This man he—he …"

Quinn filled in the blank. "He tried something nasty?"

"Yes, he did."

Quinn examined Hazel closely. "Did he hurt you? Did he actually do anything to you?"

"No, I got away."

Quinn breathed a sigh of relief. "I knew a girl once. She came to Los Angeles much like you. No friends, no family here. She had ambitions, was convinced she was going to make it. She went to meet one of these producers, executives, whatever he was. He wanted things from her, and she gave them to him. She accepted it as an ugly part of the business that she had to go along with and if it wasn't for what happened next, she might have got halfway to achieving her dream."

"Where is she now?" Hazel asked.

"She … she got caught with child. And, well, it wasn't going to be good for her career, her image. That man certainly wasn't going to take care of them, so she was sent to a, well, they told her he was a doctor, but who can really say, to take care of the problem.

She died.

She died on some back-alley table, getting a life scraped out of her.

She died because she had no choice. She couldn't go home to her family in that state. They'd never had accepted it.

Hazel, that's just one girl. I know. You've had a lucky escape this time. Don't go back. Please."

***

Two days passed in a blur, Hazel having mostly slept through it all.

In her brief waking moments, she wondered if she should beg Ricky, the owner of the diner, for her job back, but didn't know if she could face it.

Quinn had been more than patient with her, but Quinn's job alone wouldn't support them both. She'd have to start looking today.

A knock on the door disturbed Hazel from her thoughts. She opened it to Diana, clad in sunglasses and a headscarf.

"You look ridiculous," she said, shutting the door in Diana's face. "And that disguise isn't fooling anyone," she yelled through the closed door.

Diana knocked on the door again in answer.

"Go away!"

Another knock, and knowing that she would not relent, Hazel opened the door, stepping aside to let Diana in.

"I always thought I'd make an excellent spy, but you've rather ruined the notion for me now," she said, taking off her glasses and the headscarf.

"What are you doing here?"

"You don't know?" Diana asked, sitting down on the sofa.

"No."

"I told you, you need to toughen up, Hazel. And I mean it. You'll go a lot further in this business once you do. Do you think I got where I am by laying down and taking it? We women, we have to claw what we can. You have to be a bitch to get any kind of respect in this town."

"Have you ever thought that I don't want to play your game?"

"Bullshit. I want you to gather your things. No junk, that includes your clothes, you've plenty at my place. This is where you leave your old life behind. You asked me why I'm so fixated on you. Children are the real legacy, but I don't have any, so I've decided that's you."

Hazel's brow wrinkled in puzzlement. "What happened to films being your legacy?"

A wistful look passed like a cloud over Diana's face before the sun broke through, blazing in dazzling force.

"Are you coming now or should I send a car for you later? I can't imagine you've got much."

"I can't just leave Quinn—"

"And Quinn is …" Her fingers drummed on the armrest as she searched for the right word. "Your lover?"

"No, but I have responsibilities. We share the rent and utility bills. I can't expect her to take them on all by herself."

As she spoke, Diana rummaged through her pocketbook before producing her chequebook. "What's Quinn's surname?"

"Why?"

"Compensation for loss of your earnings."

"It sounds like you're purchasing me."

"No, I am assuaging your guilt. We both know that you're coming home with me, this way you'll feel a little better, although if you rather I didn't …"

She'd worked so hard to gather the money for the liner that had brought her to America.

Continued to work hard when she'd arrived in Los Angeles. And for what?

No matter how many hours she put in at the diner it was never going to be enough for her to have a home of her own.

Why shouldn't she take this opportunity? If Diana thought she was good enough.

Diana, who told her she was beautiful.

Diana, who hadn't thought twice about giving her beautiful things.

"Adler, it's Adler." Hazel watched as she wrote out the cheque, one hundred dollars, an amount that would more than cover her absence until Quinn found another roommate. In the stub she wrote; Hazel; purchase of.

I guess I deserve that for snooping.

"I'll be five minutes." Hazel left Diana cleaning her nails whilst she went to her room. Without clothes, her life didn't even fill half a suitcase. A few books, a couple of photographs, it all seemed rather pathetic. She was back in the room with Diana in less than five minutes.

Diana had left Quinn's cheque on the table, weighed down by a ketchup bottle.

"Ready?" Diana asked, her hand already on the door handle.

"Just a moment." She grabbed a scrap of paper and wrote Quinn a note explaining the cheque and where she'd be, and that she'd be in touch soon. She listened to Diana's nails rap against the door frame as she wrote, but refused to be rushed.

"Okay, I'm ready now."

Chapter Seven

"I suppose you ought to make yourself at home," Diana said. "Elsbeth will make you something to eat if you're hungry or you can help yourself. Just don't leave a mess. Aside from my own bedroom," she looked at Hazel pointedly, "there's nowhere off limits."

"I'll wait for the invitation before I come to your bed," Hazel muttered, her words dripping with bitterness.

"Yes, please do."

***

Left to explore, Hazel discovered just how cavernous Diana's home was. It wasn't just the amount of rooms, but the sheer size of them as well. Some wide enough to fit a tennis court, ceilings that stretched skywards.

There's no earthly need to have that much space above your head, Hazel thought.

The clatter of her shoes against the Spanish tile echoed around the sparsely furnished rooms. It was impossible to move silently in this house. Testament to this was the extra shadow Hazel had acquired. Elsbeth, in her sensible, clanking shoes, followed her from room to room.

Finally, Hazel's patience wore thin. "Do you have to do that?"

Elsbeth blinked twice at her from behind thick lenses.

"Did Diana tell you to do this?"

"I have a set routine I follow every day," she said in her clipped tones. "It is you that is upsetting me." She continued to stare at Hazel through the coke bottles.

"I'm sorry—"

"It is fine. They always learn my routine. You will be the same and learn to stay out of my way."

They?

Just how many strays had Diana taken in before her?

"I'm going to go in here." Hazel pointed towards a door. "Would that disturb the routine?"

"You have five minutes before I go in." Elsbeth shuffled off.

Well, Hazel thought, *I may as well go in.*

***

In stark contrast to the rest of Diana's home, in this room clutter pervaded.

Giant posters of the kind you'd find in theatre lobbies covered the walls. Each one had been lovingly placed behind glass. Hazel might have expected a room dedicated to Diana Blake pictures, but this was a shrine to Mae Joseph.

A pioneer of the silent era, every inch of space was dedicated to Mae. Her clothes adorned dressmakers' dolls. Portraits and publicity shots littered the tables.

Hazel moved carefully through the room. It was so dense here with memorabilia she had to twist and turn her body to avoid knocking anything over. Safely through the rammel, Hazel came to a space of relative clear. A sofa sat in the middle of the clearing. *That's a strange place for it,* had the briefest of times to manifest as a thought before Hazel saw the reason for its placement.

Six by six foot, the oil painting loomed over the space demanding attention, and the sofa was there to facilitate. Hazel wondered how many hours Diana spent here just looking at it.

Maybe her and Diana weren't so different; would, given the means, she not do the same?

It was an exquisite piece, brush strokes so fine they disappeared, melding into one cohesive whole.

Mae held a cigarette between her index and middle fingers, a gesture Hazel had seen Diana do this morning, and a thousand times before that.

Vases on pedestals flanked the sides, fresh flowers within them.

Hazel heard the now familiar clatter of Elsbeth's shoes.

"I have to do this room now." Elsbeth held flowers in one hand, her cleaning supplies in a bucket in the other. "Step aside, please."

Hazel moved away from the painting, watching Elsbeth as she took the flowers from the vases, replacing them with the slightly fresher ones, the others she dumped unceremoniously into a bag.

"Wasteful," Hazel said.

Elsbeth gave her an icy glare before turning back to her work. She took out a cloth and a pot of linseed oil and started to carefully burnish the already gleaming frame.

"Miss Diana requests that the flowers are replaced every day. Miss Joseph is to be honoured. She is the one who laid the groundwork, the one who made the life we have now possible." Her voice softened, taking on a faraway quality. "The picture does not do her justice. I remember when she sat for it …" She stopped abruptly as though she had said too much. "You should leave now, I have work to do and you are a disruption.

"You knew Mae!" Though Hazel knew that Elsbeth didn't want to talk any longer, her excitement overwhelmed her. "What was she like?"

"You leave, now!" Elsbeth said, putting her hands on Hazel's forearm in an attempt to steer her away.

Hazel shrugged them off. "I'll leave."

Elsbeth followed her to make sure.

***

After her expulsion from Diana's shrine to Mae Joseph, Hazel went back to her room.

She had started reading a book which reminded her of her own situation, a big house, a strange housekeeper and, although she hadn't married into this, she did feel like the neglected wife wandering the halls.

Having nearly finished the book, it occurred to Hazel that she had not eaten at all that day. She went down to the kitchen, hoping all the while she would not run into Elsbeth on the way. She made herself a sandwich, ate, and cleaned up. Still, there was no sign of Diana.

Hazel decided to fetch her book and wait for her in the reception hall.

***

It was full dark and the book was long finished before Diana returned. Hazel wanted to scream, *Where have you been? Do you have any idea how worried I've been?* She had no right to say any of this. *She's not my wife.*

"Have you been there all day?" She narrowed her eyes at Hazel. "Hmm, I thought you'd find something a little more productive to do."

"I've read a little."

"So not a complete waste of time. I, however, have spent my day cleaning up your mess." She stalked past Hazel into the lounge. "Get me a drink, would you? She sat down on the sofa, kicking off her shoes before curling her stockinged feet beneath her. "Well, are you going to ask me what I've done for you today, Hazel?"

Hazel finished mixing her a whiskey sour, debating whether to put the cherry in; she left it out. Hazel handed her the drink. Diana tapped the glass with one rose-red nail, the sharp ting that emanated from it filling the room.

"Cherry."

Hazel went back to the bar and placed a cherry in the glass. Diana reached out to take it this time and Hazel noticed that the cuffs of her jacket were damp.

"What did you do for me, Diana?"

"It's funny you should ask, Hazel." She patted the seat next to her for Hazel to sit down. "You're in. Hundred dollars a week retained on contract. Doesn't mean that you'll get work straightaway, but it will come, eventually. You'll be doing a real screen test as well."

"I thought I had already."

"That wasn't a screen test, that was Francis wanting some material to get himself off too."

"You talked to Francis?"

"No, I talked to the studio. Francis may have some sway, but he doesn't wield real power like I do." She downed her drink. "I'm going to bed."

She shoved the glass at Hazel and left. The sickly sweet smell of rum and maple tobacco, however, remained.

***

Diana was in a jubilant mood that morning, for all the airs she put on she was genuinely at home in the kitchen. The radio played softly behind the sizzle and pop of the skillet when Hazel heard the words, *"Francis Saranto—"*

She scrambled up from her chair to turn the volume up.

"Was found dead this morning at his Wilshire Boulevard home this morning. Sources say he was found in his swimming pool—"

Diana walked up behind Hazel and switched it off.

"What a shame," she said, plate in hand. "He was such a good man." Her tone was one of sadness, her mouth down-turned, but her eyes were full of mirth. "Eat up."

CHAPTER EIGHT

Hazel's illusions had been shattered. She'd never imagined that everything that followed would be so cool, calculated and clinical.

She's brought in for a personality test. She's told to walk around, light a cigarette, to just be natural, but to do it all in front of a camera. The man stood behind the camera this time didn't leer. Their only job was to track Hazel's movements, to be ready to zoom in on a smile, and to her surprise, Hazel enjoyed it.

The next step in the process wasn't so pleasant; beneath harsh lights, they scrutinised her. They measured her up and down, side to side. Thick fingers are forced into her mouth while her teeth are examined as if she's a thoroughbred horse, and it's decided that they are adequate. Next was skin. They deem the smattering of freckles across the bridge of her nose a problem. Hazel hears something about how a violet ray treatment can solve this though. Lighting and the right camera angles will remedy everything else they say.

At home with Diana, Hazel remarked on how strange the day had been. "I can't believe this is actually happening, that they'll be doing all of this for me. I mean, they don't even know if I can act."

"Doesn't matter," Diana replied. "Once they've figured out how the public responds to you and how they like you best you'll be playing that role for years. You won't need to learn another."

Hazel thought about this. At first it seemed as if it couldn't possibly be true. But then she remembered all the movies she'd watched Diana in and it dawned on her they'd all been a variation of poor girl makes good.

Was this why she clung to the idea of Diana that she'd been responding to for all these years—the possibility that she, too, could escape her humble origins?

"They'll give you background roles," Diana said. "Some small speaking parts. Monitor the fan magazines, any letters regarding you. People really do write to the studio in droves to tell them their opinions."

"What do you think my thing will be?"

"I hear they need a bitch."

***

Day after day, Hazel went to the studio, voice and poise, dance and riding, lessons after lessons with a dozen other girls who all looked remarkably alike with the exception of hair colour, of which there was a fifty-fifty split of blondes and brunettes. They ate lunch together in the studio canteen every day, this new crop of starlets. There was a surface layer of friendship coating the icy heart of the reality that they would all be willing to scrabble over each other on their way to the top. They sat apart from the featured bit players who, in turn, sat apart from all the other studio workers. The genuine stars rarely set foot in the canteen. When they did it was more a show of relatability.

Which was why Hazel immediately noticed when Diana entered the room; she strode across until she stood next to John McCarey's table.

She bent so her lips brushed against the producer's ear and whispered something; even from a distance Hazel could see the slight flicker of fear in his eyes. Diana withdrew and pointed across the room at Hazel before bending and whispering again. Hazel felt his eyes lock on her before he turned to Diana and solemnly nodded.

Satisfied, Diana loudly pronounced how good it was to see him and to say hello to his wife before flouncing off.

Until then, the exchange between Diana and John had gone unnoticed by Hazel's table mates, who now looked up to watch Diana.

Olivia, the self-appointed leader of the group, waited until Diana was safely out of the room before saying, "There should be an expiration date stamped on women, like a bottle of milk, that way you can just throw them out when they go sour."

"Why would you say that?" Hazel struggled to keep her tone even.

"Every old one hanging on denies us our chance to rise up," Olivia said with the most acetic expression on her face Hazel had ever seen. "She's had her time, it's my time now."

"That 'our' went out the window pretty quickly," Hazel said

The false smile was quickly plastered back on Olivia's face as she answered, "Oh, you know I mean that it's time for all of us." The southern accent she'd been trying so hard to repress, breaking through. "Well, would you look at that, it's time for elocution."

She passed her lunch tray to Patty, a girl whose adulation for Olivia rivalled Hazel's own for Diana. It was a privilege for her to clean away a lunch tray or carry a coat.

As they left, Hazel noticed John's eyes following her. She wasn't stupid; it wouldn't be long before he cast her in a picture.

***

Hazel wasn't wrong, within a week of the canteen incident John McCarey had cast her in a picture.

Half a line of dialogue and featured in the background of a dozen scenes. Hardly what she had envisioned. Maybe she had misjudged the scale of Diana's influence, imagined that look of fear in John's eyes.

The best thing that could happen now would be releasing her from her contract as a non-starter, setting her on her merry way.

Since living with Diana her spending had been minimal. All her food provided, shelter, transport. She could afford to go anywhere. The life Hazel was living at the moment may not be satisfying, but it was setting her up for one that could be.

Chapter Nine

"So." Quinn fiddled with the straws bobbing about in her soda. "How's it going at the studio?"

"It's really boring actually. It's like I'm being paid to do nothing."

Quinn uttered a humph which made Hazel immediately regret her words.

"And how are things with Diana?" Her voice dropped to a whisper as she leaned in closer. "Are you together?"

"No."

"I thought she was …" Her words hang in the air, and Hazel plucked them from their suspension.

"Thought she was like me."

Quinn's features darkened. "The woman bought and paid for you as if you're a dress she could just try on and then discard when she decides it doesn't suit her."

Hazel reached across the counter to give Quinn's free hand a squeeze, she didn't know what else to do. Hazel couldn't thank her for her concern, only to immediately dismiss it. Quinn seemed to understand this and so changed the subject.

"I have a new roommate."

"Already?"

"I've told you before, there's always a steady stream of stupid young girls coming here." She gave Hazel's hand a returning squeeze before letting go. "And at least this one isn't a foreigner with strange habits."

"They're not strange habits," Hazel said, lifting her chin and doing her best impression of an English aristocrat. "They are the correct and proper way of doing things that for some bizarre reason you Americans insist on doing wrong."

Quinn laughed. "Well, just to let you know, I'm not as attached to this one as I was to the foreigner."

Hazel's heart clenched at the knowledge that she could go to Quinn at any time and be taken in.

"You should visit me." The words tumbled out without any real thought. *Should I have asked Diana's permission? Surely I'm allowed guests over?*

"Hazel, I don't know about that."

"Please, you'll be able to see I'm not just some pet of hers."

That's just what you are though, isn't it?
"I'll see when I'm available," Quinn said.

"Promise you'll come, you're my only connection to normality."

"Fine, I'll come. I guess it'll be fun to poke around her house."

***

Hazel felt like a small child asking for Diana's permission for Quinn to come over.

"I don't know why you're asking me," she said airily. "It's up to you whom you choose to fraternise with."

"I'd like you to be there. Quinn doesn't exactly have a positive opinion of you."

"If everyone has a glowing opinion of you, you're not truly living."

"Please, it'll mean a lot."

"Fine, have her over for drinks."

"Thank you." Hazel wanted to go further and hug Diana but restrained herself.

"I still don't understand why you need her to like me." Her eyes narrowed as she looked at Hazel and the tight smile upon her lips betrayed her amusement. *You want validation for your own feelings for me*, it said.

She's right, Hazel thought, and she hated herself for it.

***

Diana insisted on sending a car to Quinn's to fetch her.

"If I'm going to win her over I should start now," she'd said.

The rain was pelting down a loud, steady tattoo on the windows. Hazel thought she'd left this weather behind in England. Light rippled across the sky, highlighting the fine lines around Diana's eyes. The billowing smoke from her cigarette hung in the air, enveloping her. She was an impenetrable mountain summit, one Hazel was obsessed with conquering.

Hazel watched the car turn into the drive and rushed to the door. The distant rumble of thunder mingling with the closer sound of a car door slamming, followed by the hurried clatter of Quinn's heels on stone.

The umbrella Quinn held in her hands was no match for the rain on its sideways trajectory, despite the short walk from the car it had soaked through the fabric of her dress so that it clung close to her.

"Hey, eyes up here, missy!" she said, not smiling, but a warmth in her eyes nevertheless.

Hazel pulled her into a hug, which she immediately regretted as she felt her clothes leach the dampness from Quinn's.

"Thank you," Hazel whispered.

Quinn pulled away. "Calm down, it's only drinks." She ran a hand through her ruined curls. "I hope it's the decent stuff as well. God knows she can afford it."

"I only buy the finest." Diana appeared, clutching a glass. She offered it to Quinn. "I can afford it, after all."

"Seems you can afford a great many things," Quinn said. Her eyes remained steady on Diana, but she indicated Hazel with a wave of her hand. They stared each other down a few seconds longer before Diana broke away.

"I like her, Hazel." She stalked back to the living room, beckoning them to follow.

***

Diana stood at the bar, fixing another drink. Quinn, with uncanny knowing, sat down on the sofa in Diana's usual spot. Diana took the chair opposite.

"I suppose you want to know what my intentions with Hazel are?"

She smiled warmly, as if this was an interview with a movie magazine.

Diana Blake invites us, and you, into her glamorous Wilshire Boulevard mansion.

"I see a great potential in Hazel. She—"

"You mean, she flatters you," Quinn interrupted.

"You both realise I'm right here."

Quinn and Diana ignored Hazel completely to continue sparing.

"Believe me when I say that my utmost concern is for Hazel and her career."

Hazel shot Quinn a look, which she hoped would be interpreted as *leave it.*

Quinn seemed to get Hazel's hint as she changed the subject.

"I reckon you could tell some stories."

"Darling," Diana drawled. "I am the story."

Elsbeth appeared, placing a tray of canapés on the coffee table between them all.

"Thank you, Elsbeth. I think another round of drinks is in order as well."

Quinn leant forward in her seat. "You worked with Jimmy Price." She took a devilled egg from the platter. "Tell me what he's really like." She popped the entire thing in her mouth before settling back in the chair.

"Flaccid and has to wear lifts in his shoes."

Quinn swallowed hard. "Really, and Thomas Sterling?"

"Oh, he can get hard all right, but only for those who get hard for him in return."

"I'd never have guessed, he seems like such a lady's man."

Elsbeth finished fixing the drinks, and passed them out before producing a cigarette case from her pinafore; she removed a rose-tip cigarette, handing it to Diana who put it in her mouth, Elsbeth lit it for her. In all of her time there, Hazel had never seen the ritual performed before. A show purely for Quinn's benefit. Diana gave a nod of her head towards Quinn and Elsbeth walked over to her, holding out a cigarette.

She took it, running her fingertip over the rose petal, a quick rise of the eyebrows as if to say well this is fancy before placing it between her lips.

They both settled back in their respective chairs, silently smoking.

It's going to be a long night. Hazel downed her drink and held it out for Elsbeth to refill. *Why did I bloody arrange this?*

***

The sun was too bright and there was no way to turn it off. Hazel's mouth felt as though she'd been eating sand, her stomach in knots. She looked down at the floor beside her and saw with dismay that sometime in the night she'd been sick.

"I'm never drinking again," Hazel muttered to no one in particular.

She tried to recall the night before but she may as well try to plait water. The last thing she remembered with any certainty was Diana getting a deck of cards out and Quinn shouting out that they should play a game of Oh Hell. She looked around the room, no sign of the pair of them.

Where the bloody hell are they?

Hazel removed herself from the sofa. Standing on trembling legs, she took a few tentative steps before stumbling into the coffee table, knocking the platter onto the floor.

"Shit!"

"Hazel, is that you?" Diana called. Of course they're in the kitchen, why wouldn't she be in the kitchen showing off her domestic skills to Quinn.

Equilibrium regained, Hazel set off for the kitchen. When she arrived Diana was alone.

"Where's Quinn?"

"In your room. I don't know why you insisted on passing out on the couch, there's plenty of room for the both of you in that bed." She smirked.

Hazel left Diana behind, finding Quinn sprawled on top of the covers, her breath hitching, limbs kicking out, repeating something over and over but Hazel couldn't make out the words.

"Quinn." Hazel captured a wrist as she continued to thrash. "Quinn?"

Her eyes opened wide, a glimmer of recognition in them. Then she screamed and did not stop.

Chapter Ten

Diana called the studio doctors for Quinn. They'd been waiting over an hour for them to arrive. During this time, Quinn's screams ebbed and waned. What passed for her quiet periods were full of whispered babblings. Hazel sat on the edge of the bed, just out of reach of Quinn's still kicking legs. She tried to soothe her by stroking her brow, but she recoiled from Hazel's touch.

Quinn fell back into a fitful sleep; the doctor had still not arrived.

Another hour went by, an ebb and flow of screaming and quiet. As Hazel watched Quinn softly moan and thrash, her brow furrowed and misted with sweat even in sleep, her anger at Diana could no longer be contained. Hazel decided to take advantage of the fact that for the moment Quinn seemed calm, and so slipped away.

She found Diana standing over Elsbeth, scrubbing the tiled floors.

"Where are they?" Hazel demanded.

"They'll be here soon enough—what have I told you? You need to get between the grout. We don't want a repeat of Hazel's first day here."

"Diana," Hazel pleaded. "She needs someone now."

Diana let out a sigh. "You could take Quinn to a hospital where, in her current condition, she'll be thrown into some God awful state-run facility where she'll be subjected to God knows what kind of barbaric treatments. Or you can wait."

The doctors that are coming are personal friends of mine, they'll make sure she goes to a reputable place where she can get better and I'm going to pay for it."

"She has a family."

"And they'll be thankful for this. Have patience, Hazel, they'll be here soon."

She went back to Quinn.

She was awake now, eyes wide, staring at the ceiling. Hazel approached her as you would a rabbit, careful not to startle her lest she panicked and gave flight.

"Quinn?" she asked in a voice barely above a whisper. "Quinn, how are you feeling?"

She tried to speak, but her voice was so cracked and hoarse Hazel couldn't understand her.

"Would you like some water?"

She nodded, and Hazel poured her a glass from the jug on the nightstand. She drank greedily, then held out the glass for more. Vocal chords now lubricated, she spoke, "This isn't your life."

"I've told you there's nothing to worry about."

"Hazel." She grabbed at Hazel's wrist, jerking her forward so her lips brushed against her ear as she whispered, "You don't understand. If you don't leave, you'll lose everything that makes you, you."

Hazel pulled back. "Quinn, did you ever maybe think I don't want to be me? That I crossed an ocean in order to have a new life and identity? My mum threw me out on the streets at fourteen after catching me with another girl. I fought so hard, scrimped and saved to even get to America, then had to do it all over again to get to Los Angeles. I'm not giving up now."

"This doesn't sound like you."

She was right. Even as she spoke Hazel couldn't tell if it was her or Diana talking. Everything that Hazel had said was true, but edged with a bitterness she didn't know had nested within her.

"Well, I'm happy to see that you're more yourself." Hazel's tone softened. "What happened last night?"

Quinn furrowed her brow, trying to remember. "I remember playing cards."

Hazel nodded in encouragement.

"Then you fell asleep. We played a while longer, then Diana asked if I wanted to see her collection of Mae Joseph stuff. We were talking and she was showing me things—after that I can't remember."

Quinn fell quiet again, her eyes losing focus.

Hazel heard footsteps, too heavy for Diana and Elsbeth; the men in white coats were on their way.

"Quinn, you need to talk, we'll tell them you were still drunk. That there's nothing wrong with you."

"Right through here, gentlemen," Hazel heard Diana call. "Now, I want you to take care of this young lady. She's a dear friend of mine."

"Quinn!" Hazel shook her, but she was lost within her mind.

"Has she spoken at all today?" the first man though the door asked.

Hazel started to answer but Diana got there first.

"No, all she's done is scream." She took a drag on her ever-present cigarette. "That's when she's not sat drooling."
"No, that's not true! We've been sitting talking just now. She was fine."

"Moments of lucidity can occur," the second man said to Diana. "They rarely last for long."

"Hazel, darling, come away from her."

"No, she was fine a minute ago, she'll be fine again. I'm going to take her home."

Diana stepped forward, her and Quinn's eyes locked and the screaming began again.

"She doesn't appear to be fine now," man number one said. "Please come away from her. She may be dangerous."

The second man grabbed Hazel's wrist, pulling her away from Quinn. She tore away but was quickly recaptured. The first man caught her other wrist and she was unceremoniously thrown from the room.

Elsbeth shuffled past, cleaning bucket in hand. "Easier just to let her go," she said. "Easier not to fight it."

***

From the window, drink in hand, Hazel watched the men bundle Quinn into the back of an ambulance. Her empty stomach protested every sip, but there was a certainty in her that if she could push through it, all would be well. Hazel craved the oblivion alcohol would bring, hoping it would silence the little voice in the back of her head telling her that maybe this wouldn't have happened had she been sober the night before.

"Your friend, she will be okay." Elsbeth was scrubbing the rug clean of Hazel's vomit from the night before. "When she calms down and stays that way, they will let her go. The girl is sharp, she will see this."

"I'm sorry you're having to clean up after me."

"It is alright, Miss Diana pays me well for my services and this is nothing compared to some things I've had to do for her. What's a little vomit?"

Hazel turned back to the window and took another deep swallow of whiskey. Elsbeth walked over and took the glass from her hand.

"This," she tapped the glass, "will not help you. You're a good girl Hazel, maybe you should go to sleep."

Elsbeth shuffled off, and the scream ripped through Hazel.

***

"It's only the young that can cry like this." Diana crouched beside Hazel on the floor. "The heart wrenching sobs, like the world is about to end. I remember when I used to cry like that."

Her fingers brushed against Hazel's neck as she entwined herself in her hair, pulling Hazel towards her. The kiss was different from the last, tender. Too long had Hazel been adrift in frigid waters and even as she clung on to Diana, Hazel knew that she wasn't the lifeboat she'd been waiting for. But she welcomed the possibility of being pulled under the waves. To perish in her embrace.

Diana's hand snaked down Hazel's back as her lips lingered against hers. "There's no need for tears," she murmured.

"It's not fair."

"Nothing in life is fair." She took Hazel's hand and, leading her to the couch, she sat down and patted the top of her thighs. "Put your head down."

Hazel obliged.

"You know, Hazel, I think you are the type of person who feels things deeply and I understand. Quinn's descent into madness—"

Hazel tried to raise her head, but Diana held her firmly down, stroking her hair.

"Clearly the woman's unhinged, ranting and raving like that."

"That's not like Quinn."

"Can you be sure of that? You've known her for, what, five, six months? You've no idea of her history; the woman could have been on the verge for years. One simply doesn't fall into madness pool one day without having dipped a toe in beforehand."

The more Diana spoke, the more it made sense to Hazel. What Diana was saying had to be true. Quinn had to have had this inside her all along. She cursed herself for not seeing it sooner.

"Can they help her?"

"Of course, she'll have the very best care."

CHAPTER ELEVEN

Truddi Tuttler's Tinseltown

The studio is all the home you'll ever need.

It doesn't matter what your role is, from set designer to receptionist to director.

Doctors, dentists, food and drink. They can even provide teachers for you.

In theory, you could be born, grow and be educated, then die. All without ever leaving the lot.

How else can they keep up the pace of two hundred pictures a year?

***

Hazel spent fourteen hours a day there now, the fact that every service she could ever need was there for her made it easy. But this was not out of the goodness of the studio's heart or a desire to make her life pleasant.

Olivia and Hazel were at lunch, their original group having dwindled away, when the magazine hit the table with such force it caused the Coca-Cola in Hazel's glass to slosh over.

"Looks like you're gaining attention, kid," Tom Herjervak, up-and-coming young director, said, tapping a line of text. Olivia leaned in front of Hazel to read it, blocking her view. She snorted before turning back to her meal.

Hazel picked the magazine up and read.

Truddi Tuttler's Tinseltown

Keep your eye on Hazel Sumner

English Farm Girl, 22, Steals the Show in Her First Film

I CAN'T remember any other screen newcomer who aroused as much excitement in Hollywood as Hazel Sumner did in her first picture, A Boy Must Live. The word went around before its release that we had "a young genius" in our midst.

Before the preview, I was sceptical. I get "genius" served to me regularly with the morning mail, and I take it with a grain of salt. I had seen Sumner only once-in the studio commissary, one of the new, and frankly lacklustre, crop of ingenues, and I was not impressed. But after watching her performance I admit I may be wrong about the girl.

On the screen, she has an exciting tenseness and the gift for projecting ever-changing moods …

***

Tom leant over, whispering in a conspiratorial tone, "We didn't even have to nudge Truddi into writing this."

Olivia's sour expression intensified.

"I think it's high time you moved up a peg, we want you in *Another Woman's Poison*."

"I'm in that picture!" Olivia cried.

"You can calm your britches down, that part is still yours." Tom turned back to Hazel. "Truddi thinks you have an icy British bitch air, you'll be playing opposite Olivia."

Olivia's face transformed.

"Hazel, how wonderful. Though I don't know how you're going to convince people you are anything other than an absolute sweetheart."

"I don't know, Olivia, I think you may just be able to bring it out of me."

"Save it for the camera, ladies." Tom winked at Hazel. He started to move away before turning back around. "Oh, Hazel, I'll need to see you later."

Olivia watched Tom until he was safely out of earshot.

"I'm so sorry," she said, her voice sickly sweet. "Turning you into a figure of hatred like this." She offered a poor you smile before leaving, either not realising or caring that Hazel could see the smugness dripping off her.

***

"This isn't what I wanted for you." Diana scowled at the script. "You can make a fine career out of playing women like this. But I wanted you to be adored."

"I don't mind people not liking me." *You know it's you I want to adore me.* "And I think it'll be fun playing the villainous bitch."

"It may be fun for a while, Hazel, but you won't have longevity, Ruth LuSueur is a perfect example. She had a few good years before being tossed aside."

"I don't think I've any choice in the matter."

"No," she said, her mouth set so taut Hazel could see the corded muscles in her neck. She heard the crumple of paper; Diana held the script so tightly her knuckles were as pale as the paper clutched within. "No, I suppose you don't."

She released the script from her grip, letting it fall to the ground.

Scooping it up, Hazel saw beads of red, so stark against the white, dotted on the paper.

***

Olivia had taken to this new role as featured player with aplomb. She'd bought all of the crew small gifts and was making a clear effort to learn all of their names.

It could have been cynicism talking, but Hazel thought the warmth she extruded on camera was missing from these interactions.

"I've seen this before," a young woman's voice said to Hazel.

She turned to look: red hair, brown eyes and ivory skin. The woman clutched a bundle of fabric to her chest.

Hazel felt the heat creeping up her neck and snapped her gaze back to Olivia. *Please don't be blushing, Hazel.*

"You'd think it'll only be the men who fall for this, but some of the women do too," the woman continued. Hazel felt safe enough to look at her. "Even though they are around these people everyday, some are still flattered by the attention from the beautiful movie star."

"So, you're immune to their charms?"

"I'm second-generation Hollywood. Mom and Dad have worked on pictures since the silent era. They'd tell me stories about their time on the set and so it all just became ordinary, tedious even. It's just a business."

"I've had a few people tell me that."

"One day, once the magic has worn off, you'll believe it."

"I think the magic is threadbare already."

"Well, you'll do well to remember that magic can be found elsewhere." She flashed a smile before hurrying off. Hazel watched her disappear, her frankness a refreshing tonic against the bitter liquid she'd been drinking of late.

A clash of metal directed her attention back to the set.

"Hazel?" Tom looked at her, a glint of amusement in his eyes.

"Yes."

"We're ready for you."

"Of course, sorry."

"It's alright." His tone warm and genuine. "I understand this must be overwhelming." He pointed to a soundstage done up to look like an opulent country house.

Olivia sat on the Chesterfield sofa, ready to play the poor cousin being denied her birthright by Hazel's haughty socialite.

"You know your marks?"

Hazel nodded.

The scene was a simple one, Olivia, having already been greeted by an acerbic servant, awaits Hazel, the lady of this grand house. She tells Olivia how she'll never prove how Hazel's father stole his brother's rightful inheritance and how she'll never be anything more than low class owing to her mother's lowly American status. This all climaxed with a slap by Hazel, leaving Olivia in floods of tears, wondering how on earth she'll win this battle, and the audience rooting for her.

They played the scene out. Hazel cupped her hand as she'd been instructed to, so as not to really hurt Olivia, and delivered the slap.

Olivia reeled back dramatically, falling onto the sofa as Hazel stormed off.

Olivia didn't get up as written, but her shoulders moved up and down as if racked with sobs.

"Cut!"

Olivia didn't get up.

"Cut!" Tom repeated "For fuck's sake," he muttered, then louder, "Will somebody get her up?"

The cameraman took it on himself to go over to Olivia. He placed a hand on her shoulder, spurring her into action, and she shook him off, getting up. One hand clutched to her cheek, the other raised in accusation towards Hazel, who didn't wait for the accusation to leave her lips.

"I hardly touched you." Hazel regretted going to the defence so quickly, but Olivia didn't say anything. She glared at Hazel before walking over to Tom. She whispered something to him, and he nodded in agreement.

"That's lunch, people," he called.

As the crew broke up, Hazel made her way over to Tom.

"All this because she said I really slapped her?"

"All this because she knows you were the dominant force in that scene."

Hazel didn't think much of Olivia, but would she go as far as to sabotage her by lying about assault?

Tom beckoned her closer. "Don't worry, she hasn't the clout or intelligence to do any damage. Anyone could see that you didn't come even remotely close to her. She'll go off and lick her wounds and be back playing the doe-eyed innocent. Plus she was due to take her contact lenses out for a while."

"Her what?"

"Contact lenses, she has to wear them otherwise she's practically blind, but you leave them in too long and the eyeball dries up."

"That's disgusting."

He laughed at the involuntary shudder that gripped Hazel. "Yeah, it is disgusting."

"Do you think I should try and smooth things over?"

Tom offered no more than a shrug of his shoulders in answer.

***

Hazel found Olivia at her dressing table. She watched with fascinated horror as she took out the clear discs, each nearly the size of a quarter.

"You're a braver woman than I," Hazel said.

They locked eyes in the mirror, Olivia's had taken on an unfocused look now they were bereft of correction.

"You get used to it."

"We're not in competition," Hazel said.

"Of course not." A smile skated briefly across her lips. "We new girls have got to stick together."

"I'm glad you said that, it's such a boys' club as it is."

"You are such a sweetheart." She picked up a bottle, its contents sloshing as she gesticulated. "Tom thinks we should do another take on that scene after lunch. I mean, I thought you were perfect the first time around, but who am I to argue?"

"Yes, who are we to question why?" Hazel didn't believe that Tom would ever play them off against each other, this was Olivia all over.

She tilted her head back, bringing the bottle to her right eye. As someone who'd never been able to open their eyes underwater Hazel found it oddly fascinating.

She kept the bottle to her eye for a full five seconds, then let out a scream. The bottle fell to the floor, spilling its contents, followed by Olivia.

The initial scream gave way to fast, shallow breathing., Olivia lay on the floor curled up, her whole body trembling as she whimpered, her hands clawing at her eye.

Hazel dropped to her knees, attempting to pry Olivia's fingers away from her face. Once she succeeded with that, Hazel assessed the damage. Already the skin of Olivia's eyelid was raw and swollen.

"We need to rinse this out." On the dresser was a pitcher of water. Hazel grabbed it and brought it back to Olivia, whose hands were once again covering her face. Hazel's wrestled them away once more.

"Open your eyes."

Olivia shook her head.

"Open your bloody eyes!"

To her credit she did try, but her right eye was too swollen. Hazel took her thumb and forefinger and prised it open.

There was no white left, only a fierce scarlet, the iris no longer a perfect disc, chunks of it had come away so it looked like a cog, the once vivid blue turned milky.

Hazel went to pick up the jug, paused, and tentatively put a fingertip in. It was blessedly cold.

Hazel drizzled it over Olivia's dead eye while she thrashed below her. Once Hazel finished, Olivia was soaking wet, her mouth gasping. She looked like a breached fish.

"I'm going to get you help."

Olivia reached out, imploring her to stay.

"I'm sorry," Hazel whispered.

She ran out of the room, nearly slamming into Tom.

"I heard a scream." He looked past her to the dressing room door. "You've not given her a slap for real, have you?" he said, grinning.

"She needs a doctor."

"Overestimating yourself, aren't you? No way you could have hit her that hard."

"No." Hazel's voice raised an octave. "There was something in her eyewash. Oh God, Tom, I think she's blind.

"Go back to her, I'll get help."

Hazel turned around, bracing herself to go back in, when she noticed a figure shrouded in smoke and shadow.

Diana stood, watching.

Chapter Twelve

The doctor who came was, thankfully, not the one who took Quinn away.

"What have we got here?" he asked briskly, setting down his bag.

"Her eye."

He bent down to examine it. A brief wince flashed across his face before settling back into neutrality as he turned Olivia's face back and forth.

"I rinsed her eye with water." Hazel pointed to the bottle on the floor. "It was whatever was in that eyewash."

"You did right, flushing her eye out, it could have been a lot worse."

She looked at the ruined red mess, and wondered how.

"You can go now, there's no need for you to see anymore."

***

Hazel found Diana in conversation with Tom, who immediately broke away from him to embrace her.

"Oh Hazel, you poor girl," Diana said with her usual theatrical manner. "This must be awful for you."

"Not as bad as it is for Olivia," Hazel muttered.

Diana blazed past this. "Tom told me how candescent you were in that scene and what a tragedy it'll never see the light of day."

It hit Hazel then that Olivia was not going to recover quick enough, if at all, to continue with the role. They'd have to recast.

"I'm sure I could repeat what I did today."

"We're not recasting Olivia," Tom said.

No, Hazel thought, *surely they wouldn't scrap the whole production?*

"We're recasting you."

"Tom, you said yourself that I was the best thing in that scene."

"You're taking over Olivia's role." Tom's jaw was set tight while Diana's eyes glinted with victory.

She's got exactly what she wanted.

"Hazel, I'd have thought you'd be a little more pleased. This is the role that will make you." Diana sounded downright gleeful, but at least Tom had the decency to look sheepish.

"How can I be pleased? Olivia's life is ruined."

"Tom, I'm going to see that Hazel gets home safely," Diana said.

Tom put his hand on Hazel's shoulder. "I'm sorry it happened this way too." He gave her a reassuring squeeze before dropping his hand. "She'll be well taken care of."

Quinn came to the forefront of Hazel's mind. Was she being taken care of? A surge of guilt ran though her. She'd made no effort to see how Quinn was doing.

I don't need to play the selfish bitch on screen. I am one.

"We'll shut down production for a day or so while we find a replacement for you. We'll come back better than ever."

"She'll be well prepared," Diana said, putting an arm around Hazel. "I'll make sure of that."

Tom's normally warm eyes turned to ice. "I know you will," he said to Diana before turning away from her. "Take care, Hazel."

***

Hazel was alone in her dressing room, having told Diana that she needed to gather a few things before going home. She looked at herself in the mirror, at the bleach blonde hair, the clothes she hadn't chosen, even her freckles were gone. She'd done all this and for what? A dream that had never been hers. She'd abandoned a life that although less than perfect was, at least, hers. Given time she could have met someone, lived a quiet and discreet life together.

A few more months, a few more pictures and she'd have enough to start a new life.

***

They stood outside of Diana's car, neither of them having spoken since leaving the set.

Diana fished around in her bag for her keys and, after an eternity, found them.

She shoved them into Hazel's hand.

"What do you want me to do with these?" Hazel asked, holding the keys at arm's length.

"Drive," Diana said dryly. "You do know how, don't you?"

In a way, she did. Ricky from the diner had taken her out a few times, letting her drive around the parking lot in the early hours when it was empty.

"Yes or no, Hazel?"

"Yes." Hazel got the feeling this may have been a mistake. Diana climbed into the passenger side, and soon they were out of the lot and driving down Pico Boulevard.

Diana kept glancing out the window.

"What were you doing at the studio today?" Hazel asked.

Diana glared at her; they both knew there was no reason for Diana to be there, the roles having dried up for her. After a moment she switched on her smile.

"I wanted to wish you luck." She tried, and failed, to suppress a laugh.

"What's so funny?" Hazel asked.

"If she'd kept a closer eye on her toiletries, she might still have both of them."

"Is that why you were there, to sabotage Olivia? You couldn't stand that things weren't going according to your plan?"

"You're jumping to a lot of conclusions with no proof. You should calm down."

In her growing anger Hazel's focus shifted entirely to Diana before the thud against the car's hood slammed her back to stark reality.

Chapter Thirteen

Hazel trembled behind the wheel. Diana leant over and turned the engine off. Without its racket, sounds filtered in from the street.

A woman's screams punctuated the traffic noise.

"You better see what you've hit," Diana said, examining her nails.

Hazel got out of the car. A young boy, no older than thirteen, lay on the sidewalk. Arm bent at an impossible angle. The screaming woman stood at his head; she didn't seem to be overly concerned with his wellbeing as with attracting as much attention as possible. Other than the boy's apparent dislocated shoulder he looked fine, wriggling about.

"I'm so sorry—"

"Shut up," she said. There was nothing in her eyes but surprise, as if she was expecting someone else to get out of the car. "You have any idea how much this is going to cost me? What's your name? I want to see a licence."

Hazel didn't have a licence and was about to tell the woman that when Diana appeared, holding that bloody magical cheque book. Her solution to all of her problems.

A brief glimpse of recognition flared in the woman's eyes. *Yes,* it said, *I know you have money.*

They settled into a negotiation, the woman seemingly forgetting all about the boy still on the sidewalk.

"Hey, how are you doing?" Hazel asked.

"All right, I guess. I've never ran at a car that hard before."

Before?

Hazel knelt down to whisper to him. "Did you run into the car on purpose?"

His eyes darted nervously to his mother.

"Don't worry. I won't tell."

"We know the cars, we watch them come out of the studio lot. When Mom sees one …" he trailed off.

Is there anything in this town that isn't a bloody performance?

Diana and the boy's mother were still negotiating a price, but all the hullabaloo had attracted the attention of a police officer who came strolling over. His thumb hooked into his belt, chewing gum, he looked to Hazel the epitome of a man looking for trouble. She helped the boy to his feet.

"What's going on here, ladies?" His glare bounced between them before it settled on the boy. "And what happened to you?"

Diana lifted her chin. "We saw the boy and his mother and being good citizens, we decided to help."

The officer looked at the woman for confirmation.

"My son fell. Miss Blake was so kind as to stop. She told me she'll pay for his doctor's bill. Plus enough to cover the money I'll lose missing work to look after him." She turned to Diana and smiled. "This woman is a veritable saint."

Satisfied, the cop strolled off.

"How much?" Diana hissed.

"Five hundred."

Diana scowled as she wrote out the cheque, shoving it into the woman's hand before ushering Hazel into the passenger side of the car.

"That kid threw himself at the car on purpose," Hazel said.

"You think I don't know that, whilst you accused me of maiming poor Olive—"

"Olivia."

"I saw them on the sidewalk. I watched her push him into the road."

"And you didn't think to warn me?"

"Darling, there was no chance of me getting a word in edgewise. I can only hope you've realised how silly you're being, persisting in this insistence I'm some kind of monster."

"You've spent too long in movies," Hazel muttered.

"And what does that mean?"

"That nothing that comes out of your mouth sounds real. That all your waking moments are a performance for a camera or journalist that isn't there. And with each passing year that camera spends a little less time on you, that reporter is less likely to ask you for a quote."

"You ungrateful little bitch." Diana smiled as she said this, as if pleased with Hazel's nasty streak.

That approval sickened Hazel.

***

Truddi Tuttler's Tinseltown

HOLLYWOOD, May 15—Olivia Jackson's tragic accident will leave an enormous hole in TKA's production schedule. She was set to star in Changing Season with Thomas Sterling. The studio had also bought The Intimidation Game for her. Replacing the little Jackson girl is going to be a mighty hard task. It's a great pity that Olivia didn't check what was in that bottle …

***

Hazel and Diana didn't speak for days after their argument.

Hazel was gone from six a.m. to six p.m., sometimes later, the shooting schedule for *Another Woman's Poison* having to make up for the delays and cost of Olivia's 'accident'.

In the days since the incident, as it had become known, Hazel had yet to see the redheaded woman again.

Hazel decided to ask Tom if he knew who she was.

His lips curled in a knowing smile. "I know her. Why do you want to know who she is?"

"She was friendly to me on my first day. I wanted to say thank you."

"Kat."

"Kat?"

"Short for Katarina, but she's been Kat since she was a kitten."

"You've known each other for that long?" How well did he know her? A pang of disappointment stabbed at Hazel.

"Our folks worked together, we grew up running around the studio lots."

"I should have guessed you were second generation Hollywood."

"Yeah?"

"Yes, because you're so normal and relaxed about everything."

This earnt another dose of his warm laughter.

"Kat works in costuming."

An image of her hands measuring and smoothing fabrics rose unbidden in Hazel and she almost forgot that Tom was still talking.

"She shouldn't have been on the set that day."

"Maybe she wanted to have a look at you, Mr. First-time Director." Hazel tried to sound jovial, but Tom must have sensed her disappointment beneath it as he hurriedly added, "We're not together, she's like a little sister to me."

Hazel nodded, pleased with this information, but then it hit her.

He thinks that I'm jealous of Kat, not the other way around.

"I don't care who you date," Hazel said, trying to deflect any hopes on his part. "I like you like a brother." Hazel cursed herself, all she'd achieved was to make it all feel rather awkward.

Tom laughed. "Hazel, there's no need to explain yourself."

"I really do consider you a friend, Tom."

"My next picture I'll try to have Kat working on it." His normally bright features darkened. "It might go some way to breaking whatever hold Diana has over you."

"She doesn't have a hold of me."

His silence was more damning an answer than any words.

***

Hazel had been in search of a book to read when, breaking her promise to wait for an invitation first, she wandered into Diana's room. She looked longingly at the bed where Diana took her lovers. Before she could stop herself she laid down on the bed. Burying herself in the scent clinging to her pillows, she stretched out, knocking over the clock on the side table.

"Shit!"

It had fallen behind the table, stuck between it and the wall. She freed the clock and placed it back. Hazel was just about to retreat back to her own room when she noticed something else. A book, leatherbound.

It was old, yellowed, and smelled strongly of musk. Hazel thought it would fall apart completely.

When she opened it, several pages fluttered to the ground. She gathered up the loose pages—the gaps within the spine made it clear that many more had been lost over the years-and went downstairs to read.

January 8th '96

I'm no longer allowed to go into town by myself.

Father doesn't like the way men look at me, mostly because they look at me the same way he does.

It could be any day now that he'll give in and take from me that which he believes is his to take.

What he doesn't know is that I've already given it to David; he's promised to marry me. Promised that we'll move to the city. I'd do anything to escape this house even if it means marrying that disgusting man.

June 16th '97

Our trip to the city was a wonderful one, at first. We went to a vaudeville theatre which had a projector. It's not like the kinetoscope I've seen before. This was a screen big enough for a group of us to look at.

I looked at the faces filled with wonder around me gazing up adoringly.

I want people to look at me this way.
David ruined it when we got back to the boarding house by striking me in the ribs. I think they're broken.

It's my 17th birthday

The slam of the door brought Hazel back to the now.

She shoved the diary behind the cushions; she couldn't explain to Diana how she'd come in possession of it.

"Why do you look so sad?" Diana said, sitting down opposite her.

"No real reason. I've just been thinking, is all."

"Maybe that's a pastime you shouldn't engage in if this is what it leads to."

Hazel nodded, she couldn't get Mae out of her mind. At least she knew that somehow, she had escaped. Had a career, bought this house. She had an idea of why Diana admired her so ardently.

"Diana?" she asked carefully, softly. "You were married, once. What was he like?" Hazel braced for a rebuke for asking such an impertinent question.

Instead Diana's eyes softened. "I wasn't the first woman to find herself chained to a brute. And I certainly was not the last either. He beat me. Forced himself on me when I said I didn't want to." She paused. "Maybe I'm not a very nice person at times, Hazel, but this is what I've had to learn to do to survive in this world."

Hazel nodded in understanding. It was a cruel world and Diana had had no choice but to become cruel herself to survive in it.

Maybe, Hazel thought, *if I showed her it didn't have to be this way, I can make her love me.*

***

Diana had a paramour, the recently widowed Raymond Blaine, and unlike the men she'd brought home every other night, he was a few years her senior.

She looked at him like a puppy clinging to any person who showed them even a modicum of affection.

She has become me.

He sprawled out over her furniture, all long sharp limbs, while he waited for her to finish getting ready.

"What are you going to be doing tonight, Hazel?"

He said *what* but the waggle of his eyebrows suggested he really meant *who*.

"Just me and a book."

"You could have your pick of men, and if you happen to get in trouble, it's easily fixed."

"Are you speaking from personal experience?" Hazel thought of Quinn's friend, dying on some back-alley quack's table.

"Well, I've not been caught out yet."

"Caught out with what?" Diana was at the door, a vision in dusky silver which looked as if it had been made molten and poured over her, such was the way it clung to her breasts and hips.

Thank God, Hazel thought, *that Raymond's eyes are fixed on Diana so he can't see the hunger burning in mine.*

The perfect gentleman, he rose to cross the room and, taking her hands in his, he placed a kiss where neck met jawline. "You look beautiful," he said, and Hazel knew he meant it.

"You haven't answered my question." Diana said.

"Just a silly conversation me and Hazel were having."

"Hazel will tell me." Diana looked at her expectantly.

"He was telling me how marvellous back-alley abortions are. No one need ever be caught out with an unexpected child again."

"Diana, tell Hazel that she should go out and have a little fun. Maybe if she had a good screw, she wouldn't be so uptight."

Diana looked smugly at Hazel. "You're not wrong, Raymond."

***

Hazel had fallen asleep fully dressed on top of the covers, the book she'd been reading covering her face, when she was awoken by the sound of squealing tires. She went to the window just in time to watch Raymond get out of the driver's side door, a bottle in his hand, and stagger around to the other side to open the door for Diana.

She was studier on her feet, though not by much, than Raymond, and he had to put his arm around Diana's shoulder to steady himself as they stumbled to the front door. How on bloody earth had they managed to get home without wrapping the car around a palm tree?

Their drunken voices filled the house.

"Come on, darling, what was I supposed to do? She came onto me," Raymond slurred.

"Not going to the coat check room and putting your dick in her mouth would have been one option!"

Hazel crept to the top of the stairs. Raymond was face down on the chaise longue next to the telephone, already snoring.

Diana stood glaring at him a moment before turning her eyes towards the staircase and Hazel. Embarrassed, she hurried back to her bedroom, the sound of Diana's footsteps not far behind.

Diana entered the room, closed the door behind her and leant against it, that silver dress showing every curve. The slight sheen of sweat shone in the hollow of her throat. Hazel wanted nothing more in that moment than to dip her tongue in and taste her.

"So, why don't you show me what you can do?"

Hazel took a hesitant step forward, then froze. Her throat felt tight, her head light. This had to be some sort of game, a trick. Diana Blake, goddess, was not stood in front of her asking to be taken.

"What's the matter, Hazel, afraid you can't satisfy me?"

Hazel went to Diana, put a hand on her cheek and leant in.

"No, I don't want that." Diana placed a hand on Hazel's shoulder and pushed down. Hazel, with a reverence normally reserved for royalty, dropped to her knees.

She slipped a hand around one silk-stockinged calf and slowly moved upwards, gasping when she came to the bare skin of Diana's upper thigh. She revelled in the softness she found there a moment, tracing featherlight circles with her thumb, before her hand continued its journey upwards until she could hook her fingers into Diana's panties. She pulled them down in one swift movement, helping Diana, still in her black heels, step out of them. Hazel pushed the silver satin of Diana's dress up to her hips. Diana grasped the material, keeping hold of it whilst Hazel lifted one of Diana's legs over her shoulder. She stopped again for a moment, breathing Diana in before nuzzling into her soft curls. She ran her tongue over Diana's centre, and was rewarded with a sigh. Hazel continued, slowly, deliberately, listening carefully to Diana's moans, her breathing.

Sensing that Diana was close, Hazel quickened her strokes. The flood of her own arousal was almost painful. She wanted desperately to put her hand between her own legs, to sate her own need, but instinctively knew that this would displease Diana; this was her pleasure alone.

Diana's hips bucked as she climaxed. Hazel placed her hand on Diana's waist, holding her close as the last waves of pleasure rippled through her.

Once her breathing had slowed, Diana pushed Hazel away and pulled down her dress. She looked down at Hazel, who still gripped the black silk panties tight in one hand, and gave a soft throaty chuckle before leaving. The click of the door closed like a shot through Hazel's heart.

Chapter Fourteen

On their evenings alone, Elsbeth and Hazel had fallen into a strange companionship. Two women who both crossed oceans to escape their previous lives only to both end up under Diana's rule.

How was it that this woman had become the centre of both their worlds?

"Why do you stay?" Hazel asked Elsbeth as she cut and glued the rose petals for Diana's cigarettes.

"It's my job."

"But surely at your age you want to retire, to relax? Not run after a woman who is half your age."

She let out a little snort of derisive laughter. "I came to America forty-one years ago, Miss Diana was the first, the only person to show me kindness."

Hazel brow furrowed as she did the maths. "You were waiting a long time."

"What do you mean?"

"If you came over in 1899 that would have made Diana four years old."

She looked up from her work. "Time all blurs together. There must have been another before her."

"Mae?"

She nodded. "Yes, Mae."

Hazel ventured forth carefully. Elsbeth had never spoken so freely before, she didn't want to scare her off.

"Did Diana know Mae?"

A nod. Hazel wondered if Elsbeth was merely an acquisition of Diana's, a living remnant of Mae's life for her to keep clean the rest of her collection.

"Mae was my everything."

Elsbeth noted Hazel's raised eyebrows.

"Not in that way. No, it was a kinship. This world can be hard for a woman. We navigated it together, protected one another."

"It must have been hard when you lost her."

Her expression was curiously pensive. "She is still with me every day in many ways."

Was the shrine to Mae more Elsbeth than Diana? That first day Hazel had stumbled upon it, Elsbeth had treated it with a reverence that went far beyond that of a mere employee. Was she the reason that Diana smoked the same rose-tipped cigarettes as her predecessor, had Elsbeth moulded Diana to be a replacement for her?

"When did you meet Diana?"

Her face went blank a moment, Elsbeth was taking the time to choose her words.

"We found Diana nineteen years ago, you'd never seen such a pathetic creature, dirty, drifting from bed to bed just so she'd have somewhere to sleep, it's a wonder that she hadn't been murdered and left in a gutter like the trash she was."

The disconnect between the way she spoke of the Diana of the past and the Diana of today was startling.

"She was so desperate." She shot a wary look towards Hazel. "Not like you. You have a quiet desperation to you, but only where Diana is concerned. That Diana had a stench as strong as a polecat. She came from a city slum and it showed. Mae came from the country, a hard life, yes, but one that bred strength and character.

The day at Hazel's former apartment, when Diana had tried to tell her that she remembered being on the farm, came flooding back, it now looked like an attempt to rewrite her history to match Mae's.

"And Diana now?"

"Miss Diana has grace and dignity, she would never debase herself."

That's it, Miss Diana and Diana are two separate persons in Elsbeth's mind.

As for Diana not abasing herself, well, as time wore on that seemed to be less and less the case.

She was perfectly willing to ignore Raymond blatantly stepping out with any young women that would have him, so long as he at least paid Diana a little attention once he grew bored with them.

"I'm going to bed now," Elsbeth said abruptly.

Hazel's luck had run out, Elsbeth got up and for the first time her age and fragility hit Hazel. What could Diana have done to earn this woman's respect so that she'd be willing to spend the rest of her life slaving over her?

***

Truddi Tuttler's Tinseltown

ANOTHER WOMAN'S POISON has been released, but it is not the success that the studio hoped it would be.

Following Olivia Jackson's accident, the mind-boggling decision was made to switch Hazel Sumner from the supporting role of the icy English socialite to the starring role of plucky American underdog. With Lauren Parker brought in to fill the gap.

Both women fail to excite.

Worse, the footage of Hazel and Olivia in their one scene together has been seen by the studio execs and, according to a trusted source, was electric, and now they are livid, wanting to know why it was that Hazel's role was recast and not Olivia's. What is for certain is that the whole debacle has put a damper on Hazel's raise to stardom …

***

Diana, for her part in all of this, remained unmoved.

Even as Hazel was thrown back into the pool of bit players, she refused to acknowledge she was wrong.

"It's not your fault the picture flopped," she said, sprawled out on her sun lounger, wearing a two-piece and a wide-brimmed hat to protect her from the sun. "That idiot they got to replace you brought the whole thing down."

"I could have been great in that role."

"But Hazel, who would have loved me after that?"

"You mean me?" Hazel asks.

Diana took a sip of her drink and lit a cigarette.

"You mean me, right?"

She took a drag of the cigarette then, tired of it already, stubbed it out, laid back on her lounger and pulled the brim of her hat down.

***

"Wake up!" Diana's voice rang in Hazel's ears, she was leant over the bed, her lips inches from Hazel's.

"I'm up."

She backed away and Hazel saw that in her hand she clutched a piece of paper.

"This came for you." Diana shoved the letter at her, already crumpled and read. She didn't need to read it. By Diana's reaction to it Hazel knew it was a termination of contract, a cursory glance confirmed it.

"Guess I can go back to sleep." She tossed the letter aside.

"You are not lounging in this bed all day."

Diana yanked the sheet away.

"You're not entirely to blame, the studio put no work into you. They could never have had any intention for you to progress further. That picture was a test for Tom. And this!" She pinched Hazel's thigh. "Good God, there's healthy and then there's fat."

"Fuck you."

"Huh, well I suppose it suits you to a fashion, but your hair and skin are so dull and lifeless. I should have had a routine set up for you from the beginning."

She'd seen Diana's routine, bowls of ice and scrubbing with witch hazel. A diet of black coffee, cigarettes and alcohol.

Hazel was on her way with the alcohol aspect of it; drinking had become a way of coping with the tedium. Elsbeth always retired early, leaving her alone, and there was seldom little else to do.

Since Hazel had been with the studio and in Diana's web, she'd not dared to go to any of the clubs on Sunset Strip where women like her frequented, for fear of being recognised.

"Get up."

"Why am I still here?" Hazel muttered as she got out of the bed and walked to the bathroom. "I've money enough to just up and leave. Go to New York, stay there a while before going to London. The war in Europe can't last forever."

"What are you doing?" Diana asked her as she threw on some slacks and a shirt.

"I'm going to Sunset Strip," Hazel said.

Diana's eyes widened in horror. "No, you can't do that to me."

"I can't do anything to you, hence the reason I need to go to the Strip. Also, you need to let go of this idea that I'm going to be some kind of successor."

"How are you even going to get there?"

"Believe it or not, Diana, but I managed to traverse Los Angeles without you before. I'm getting a fucking cab."

Hazel was out the door and walking down the street before it occurred to her that she should have called the cab before leaving the house. It'd take twenty minutes to walk to the drugstore from here, an unpleasant prospect in this heat, not to mention she'd become spoiled, unused to walking any great distance.

Hazel must have been walking for fifteen minutes. The sweat was starting to drip down her back. If she did make it to the Strip, she'd hardly be at her most attractive.

She heard a car slowing down beside her, and Diana pulled up.

"Get in."

Hazel carried on walking, determined to ignore Diana.

"Please."

A few more minutes and she'd be at the drugstore and able to ring for a cab.

"I'm sorry!"

This stopped Hazel, never had she thought Diana capable of uttering those words.

"I'm sorry. I'm sorry that I don't treat you as well as I should. That I take advantage of the fact that you have feelings for me that I could never return, but Hazel, please get in the damn car."

Hazel got in, slamming the door behind her.

"You look fucking awful," Diana said.

"Right, I'm going." Hazel reached for the door handle but Diana's hand on hers stopped her.

"You have needs, Hazel, and I shouldn't have mocked you for them, or let Raymond say that maybe you wouldn't be so uptight if you had a fuck."

Hazel stared blankly ahead as Diana ploughed on. "Although he's right, isn't he? That's why you're going to Sunset, to find a woman who'll take you to bed?"

Hazel's face burned.

"You understand why I can't let you do that though, don't you?"

"The LA police have no jurisdiction on Sunset and the Sheriff's department pretty much leaves it alone. It's safe—"

"It's not safe, Hazel. There's still the possibility of raids, reporters, the indiscretion of your lovers."

"I don't have a career to protect."

"I'm going to take you somewhere you can let off steam with no repercussions."

***

The part of town Diana drove to was not familiar to Hazel, but seemed respectable enough. They pulled up outside of a Victorian style house.

"What are we doing here?"

"I told you. You have needs, Hazel. Your particular brand requires that they be dealt with tact and discretion."

She looked at the unassuming house. In the time they'd been parked there, three men had entered and two had exited. Realisation dawned.

Diana had brought her to a brothel.

"She's booked and paid for."

"I'm not going in there!"

Diana grabbed Hazel's hair, bringing her closer to her. Hazel felt hot breath on her neck, Diana's other hand was on Hazel's waist, locking her into a faux lovers embrace.

"Are you sure?" Diana whispered. "How long has it been?"

Hazel's breath hitched, her heart started to race, and she leant forward to capture Diana's lips. She pushed Hazel away with a smirk on her face, satisfied at how easily she manipulated her.

"Or you can come home with me, play cards with Elsbeth then retire to a cold, empty bed."

Diana was still tantalisingly close. Perfume filled Hazel's nostrils, the feel of her hair as it brushed against Hazel's bare arm made her shiver. Every time this woman was close to Hazel her body betrayed her.

"Go inside and have a little fun. They're expecting you."

She leaned across Hazel, opened the car door and all but pushed her out.

The walk to that house was the most shameful of her life.

***

The woman who greeted Hazel was the double of Joan Blondell.

"First time at Marlene's, honey?" the woman asked softly.

Hazel nodded.

"Don't you worry, honey, Diana will take good care of you."

"Yes," was all Hazel could manage. How could Diana berate her for imagined indiscretions, then turn around and use her real name to arrange this?

The Joan lookalike took Hazel's hand and led her up the stairs. "We don't get many women, but it's not unheard of." She opened the door and gestured towards the bed. "Just you wait here, honey, Diana will be with you in just a moment. Have fun!"

She was gone before Hazel could ask what was going on.

A voice called from the adjoining bathroom, "Make yourself at home, darling, I'm just freshening up." The tone and cadence of this voice was eerily familiar to Hazel.

Hazel sat on the bed's edge. With each moment that passed, her heartrate quickened, she hadn't felt so nervous since that first morning at Diana's house when she thought she was in Diana's bed.

Diana? Surely it had to be some kind of a sick coincidence that this woman's name was also Diana.

The door opened; dark hair tumbling down over pale shoulders, blue eyes narrowed in that intense gaze that had haunted Hazel for years.

"Who are you?"

"I'm Diana Blake, darling."

Chapter Fifteen

The woman was a superb actress, all of Diana's mannerisms and quirks perfectly replicated. It was not the real Diana that Hazel had come to know. This was the Diana of the screen and newsreel. The exaggeration of the person. The woman Hazel had spent years fascinated by.

Hazel had heard of these places before but never thought them real, places where you could spend a few dollars and have a night with your favourite movie star. A night of fantasy fulfilled.

The fake Diana sat on the bed beside Hazel. She picked up a cigarette case and took out a red-tip cigarette. Sitting this close to her, Hazel could see that it wasn't the soft rose petal of the real Diana's cigarettes, but the paper was coloured red so haphazardly that white flecks showed through.

"Don't be nervous, darling." The woman placed a hand on Hazel's thigh, her soft hair brushing against Hazel. It was like being back in the car, even the perfume was the same.

She lifted Hazel's chin up to kiss her, and it was so warm and convincing Hazel couldn't help but melt into it.

The woman pulled away from Hazel, getting up to stand before her.

Hazel's first instinct was to apologise for her transgression, instead the woman undid the belt on her robe, letting it fall to the floor. She stood before Hazel in all her flawless glory.

Hazel didn't know how long she sat dumbfounded before the woman leant in and whispered into her ear.

"It's okay, just enjoy the illusion." Gone were the clipped, mid-Atlantic tones, replaced by a southern English accent.

She straightened up, and she was Diana again.

"Why don't you take your clothes off, darling, and then we can have some real fun?"

"I can't." Hazel's heart felt as if it were being squeezed and could pop at any moment. This was the cruellest thing that Diana had ever done, Hazel could picture her laughing.

Pathetic, degenerate Hazel!

She thinks she can have me. I'll pay for her to have a pale version of me.

"I've been paid whatever we do," the woman said, letting the act drop again. "But you're a lot cuter than my usual clientele."

This was what Hazel needed, however much Diana thought she'd like the performance, this woman was not Diana.

At first glance she might have appeared to be, but her eyes were a few shades darker, her lips slightly fuller. The illusion broken, Hazel stood up and stripped, before lying back on the bed. The woman climbed on top of her, peppering kisses down her chest and stomach before settling between her legs.

***

"Your time's up sweetie," fake Diana said as she gently shook Hazel awake.

Hazel stretched and yawned. Her whole body felt lighter, every bit of tension gone. The woman placed a kiss on her forehead.

"I want to stay here forever," Hazel murmured, burying her head beneath the pillow.

"Believe me, sweetie, I would not mind that at all."

Hazel started to come round properly, realising that she wasn't in Diana's bed.

"I had a lot of fun but please don't tell anyone I broke character. They really don't like it when we do that. Ridiculous really, as if anyone could really believe I'm the real Diana Blake."

"You do a good turn as her, but—"

"But, not quite," she finished for Hazel. "I felt bad seeing that terror in your eyes when I walked in. You looked so confused. I'm sorry it wasn't what you expected. I think men don't stop to think too closely about whether it's real or not. They're in and out before I can even feel them most times."

Hazel felt like saying that she hadn't been expecting anything, but remained silent.

The woman reclined back; her hair pooled around her head on the pillow. "Get yourself dressed, and darling?"

"Yes."

"Feel free to come back anytime."

***

Diana had sent a car to wait for her. The driver sneered at Hazel as he held the door. They rode in silence, and it was dark when Hazel arrived back at Diana's.

"Better?" she sneered.

"Certainly a better kisser than you," Hazel said, walking straight past Diana and up to her room.

***

Harsh light streamed through Hazel's eyelids. She tried to lift her hand to shield her eyes but couldn't.

Soft leather cuffs encircled her wrists; she wasn't in her bed either.

She was on a leather recliner. Hazel tried to scream but her mouth was full of cotton and the heavy numbness that comes with Novacaine.

"You didn't give her enough, she's waking up."

"It's done anyhow, she'll be tender for a few days so—"

"Yes, I remember from when I had mine removed. Get her out of that thing."

A man Hazel recognised as the studio's dentist hastily unshackled Hazel's wrists.

"You know I don't like doing this procedure anymore. It causes so much damage down the line."

"You're getting paid, aren't you?"

Thick fingers probed Hazel's mouth, removing blood-soaked cotton.

"What have you done?" Hazel tried to ask, but what came out was a garbled mess.

A silver tray glinted on the table, on it were two teeth, their long roots still bloodied.

CHAPTER SIXTEEN

Truddi Tuttler's Tinseltown

Dec 9th 1939

HAD A red-letter day at TKA. Lunched with the king of the lot, Raymond Blaine. Alone, fortunately, so I ask him the $61 question; is he going to marry Diana Blake? They've been seen together several times out on the town. He laughed before carrying on eating his lunch of sliced tomatoes and lemonade.

Rumour has it Blaine spends most of his time on *The Black Rose* set. Could the reason be that lovely redhead working in the picture, or is he just taking an interest in her career?

***

Elspeth had bought Hazel an ice pack to help with the swelling.

"You're going to look fabulous, cheekbones to die for." Diana sat by Hazel's bedside. "You'll thank me soon enough."

She brushed her fingertips down the side of Hazel's face lightly, but not lightly enough to prevent Hazel from wincing. Diana chuckled at this, evidently finding Hazel's pain amusing, before getting up.

"Where are you going?" Hazel asked.

"Raymond is taking me to New York for Christmas."

She stole my teeth and now she's abandoning me to swan off to New York. What does she expect me to do, sit and play cards with Elsbeth?

"When I get back I'm going to present you anew. New face, new hair, maybe a new name! They love a name the star competition in *Screenplay* magazine. Personally I think they're old hat, but they do make the public warm to you. Everybody likes to think they're a part of the process. This will all wait until the New Year though."

She lingered by the doorway.

"Isn't it exciting. Hazel? I'm going to fix everything for you."

***

It's in all the papers about Raymond and Diana. It makes a good story, the handsome widower finding love again. They'd never mentioned the dozens of other lovers he had, even though he made no effort to hide them.

Hazel was going crazy; she could only take so much more of Elsbeth's company.

"You know you don't have to stay with me," Elsbeth said, putting down a card. "Without Miss Mae here you should go and have some fun while you can."

It had become increasingly common for Elsbeth's words to belie a deeper meaning. Hazel thought her mind must be going, she sometimes called Diana Mae. The fury flashing in Diana's eyes when Elsbeth made that mistake was terrifying. Any mention of Mae in front of Hazel seemed to incite a rage. Hazel would feel guilty if she was just to leave Elsbeth alone and wondered, not for the first time, if Elspeth had any friends she could call to come over and keep her company.

"Once Diana has her way with you, you won't be yourself. You've five, six months before that happens. So go, have fun."

"Elsbeth, what do you mean once 'Diana has her way'? Why is she so focused on me?"

Elsbeth blinked dumbly at Hazel. "You don't have to stay here with me, you should go and have fun."

Hazel reached across the table and squeezed her hand. "I'm having fun here."

Elsbeth smiled and played another card.

***

It was just past midnight, and Elsbeth was sleeping. Hazel sat in Diana's car, thinking of the two places she could go.

Having made her choice she started the car.

Chapter Seventeen

Hazel had thought of going to the Strip, but Diana was right, she couldn't risk it. So she went to the one other place she could think of.

Even at half one in the morning, there was a constant stream of men coming in and out of Marlene's.

What have you become? Quinn's voice rang in her ears.

Diana joined the cacophony. *You're pathetic. I knew you wouldn't be able to keep away.*

"Enough!"

She slammed the car door and strode up to the house. She passed a trio of men, the glowing ends of their cigarettes illuminating one man's furrowed brow. A glint of recognition followed by disappointment of why Hazel, star of one momentous flop, bit player in a dozen or so mediocre pictures, would be here. It couldn't be the real Hazel, but who would want to pay for a night with a Hazel Sumner when there was a Diana Blake or Loretta Young available?

Hazel stood in the hallway, her heart racing, but not like last time when Diana had wound her up like a clockwork toy, tension so tight it had no choice but to find a release. She wasn't expected now, and she would be forced to ask for the fake Diana herself. The same Joan Blondell lookalike who'd greeted her the first time came to her.

"Back for more?"

Hazel nodded and swallowed hard "Is Diana here?" she asked, her voice cracking.

"Diana Blake? Honey, she's out of town, you must have seen in the papers that she's in New York. How about we find you someone else?"

"How could she be in New York?" Hazel asked before stupidly realising that it was all part of the illusion. How could Diana be ready to fulfil someone's fantasy if she's not in LA?

"It's fine, I'll come back another time."

Hazel turned to leave, only to catch the eye of a small blonde.

"Are you Hazel?" she asked. Unlike Joan, this woman's eyes still held the spark of youth and hope. She had not yet resigned herself to the fact that this was her life.

There was still the hope that someone would see her potential and take her away from this place.

"Come with me."

"Thank you, but no."

The young woman reached for Hazel. "If you want to forget about Diana, you should really come with me." She gestured with a slight tip of her head up the stairs. Understanding, Hazel followed.

Once safely behind a locked door, the girl said.

"You're looking for Laura?"

"Is that Diana?"

"She told me that if you ever came back to give you this." She went to the bedside table and took a bible out from the drawer.

"I think I'm far beyond saving," Hazel quipped. She was gifted with a stare as the blonde plucked a note from its pages. Hazel took it, and written on it was a name and address. What had made Diana, no Laura, so certain she would come back?

"Thank you," Hazel said as she moved towards the door.

"I'm sorry, but—" The girl held her hand out. "Every minute I've spent with you is a minute I could have been making money."

Hazel dug in her purse. Finding several notes, she shoved them into the girl's hand. It was probably more money than the girl had seen in her life, and Hazel wondered how much of it the girl would get to keep for herself.

"I can see why Laura was so keen to see you again."

She took all but one of the bills, smoothing them before placing them between the pages of the bible. The girl was more savvy than Hazel credited her.

"Where are you from?"

"Colorado."

"You should take that money and get on a train."

"I'll be out of here soon enough. The other girls are pale imitations. I have what it takes to be the real deal."

Hazel wanted to grab the girl, to scream at her, whatever it would take to make her realise that would never be the case, but the resolution and fire in her eyes told Hazel it would be pointless to even try. She'd seen that exact look in Olivia's eyes before, she'd had it that day in the studio canteen when she'd been fantasising about dethroning Diana. Olivia was safe back home now, but her time in Hollywood had cost her dearly.

What would it cost this girl?

***

Hazel had always thought the apartment she and Quinn had shared was depressing. Laura's building, though, was squalid. The brickwork was fire damaged and the smell of damp prevailed throughout the hallways.

Hazel knocked at the door.

"Who is it?" Laura said through the door.

"It's Hazel."

The sound of three locks clicking and a chain sliding across before the door opened.

"Can I come in?"

The apartment belied the outside, fastidiously clean and freshly decorated.

Laura smiled. "Do you want a drink?"

"I'm fine, thank you."

Laura sat on the couch, folding her hands into her lap. "I knew you'd come back at some point. I enjoyed our evening together. I think you did too. You don't have to feel guilty about it."

Laura's words had the opposite effect, flooding Hazel with guilt. She'd come here tonight not because she'd missed Laura, but because she was missing Diana.

"So, I guess you have a few days off."

"Yeah, it's kinda nice having Christmas off. You'd think that at this time of year men would want to spend time with their families. But no, they're still knocking on that door."

"How long have you been in LA?" Hazel said, but really meant how long had she been playing the role of Diana Blake?

"Oh, I came over on the boat in '33. I don't know what I was thinking about, coming to America. I suppose, in retrospect, with the war going on, I made the right decision. America isn't going to get involved in it all, and

Hitler can't reach over here, so ..." Laura shrugged her shoulders. "What about you?"

"I've not been here that long."

"Did you always want to be an actress?"

"I guess I just wanted what you did, a different life."

"Well, I hope you succeed where I failed. This city, it's full of snares, and before you know it you're trapped. Though I must admit I'm better paid than I ever was back in England."

Hazel glanced around the apartment.

Laura laughed. "Obviously, I'm not spending what I make on living here. I'm saving up. When I first came over, I stayed in this beautiful little guest house. Two English ladies ran it. Eve and Addy? Something like that. Anyway, that's what I'm going to do. I'm going to buy a house, run my own business. I'm getting too old for this game. Heck, Diana is getting too old for this game. Used to be that I'd get four, five Johns a night. I'm lucky if I get that in a week now."

Hazel looked at Laura and, for the very first time, didn't see Diana.

"You love her, don't you? It's not lust or infatuation, you truly love her. But you don't want to. Is that the reason you went to Marlene's? To cleanse yourself? Get it out of your system?"

"I didn't know. When you walked into the room, my heart stopped. I was so angry that Diana would do that to me ..."

"I think you better tell me more. I also think that I want a drink in my hand while I listen to it."

After spending so long in Diana's company, Hazel had expected her to produce a bottle of something alcoholic. To her surprise, Laura went straight to the kitchenette and put the kettle on to boil.

"Do I need to ask if you want a cup of tea?"

***

Laura listened as Hazel recounted her life as it was since she'd met Diana. She had expected Laura to be as shocked and horrified as she had been at the forced removal of her teeth, but she calmly placed her cup on the table and opened her own mouth to show Hazel.

"Had to have them taken out to better match Diana's jaw line. This isn't my real nose either. I know this isn't what you want to hear, but you will never be happy as long as you bind yourself to her."

Hazel stared blankly ahead, chewing on the inside of her cheek. How could she explain to Laura how Diana held everything she was in her hands? That even when Diana threw her to the ground and crushed her under her heels, she could never leave? The pull was too strong, a steel chain bound her to Diana and she would follow wherever she was led.

Laura reached over, her thumb wiping a tear away. A tear she hadn't known she'd shed.

"You know what I'm saying is true," Laura said, gently pulling her into a hug. Hazel turned, capturing her lips in a kiss. She needed her to be quiet, she needed to believe it was Diana burying her fingers in her hair. Diana who moaned against her lips as her hand made her way up her thigh and between her legs.

With the first thrust, Laura broke away.

"Hazel!" The name came out breathy and pleading, devoid of accent.

Was this what her name would sound like said by Diana in the throes of passion? She built her rhythm, rewarded by her name being called out again and again. Until she felt Laura's body tighten, before collapsing against her.

Hazel withdrew, going straight to the sink to wash her hand; Laura came up behind her, nuzzling at her neck.

"That was—"

"I have to go." Hazel returned to the sofa, picking up her bag. "I'm sorry, I never should have come here." Standing at the door, she added, "I hope you get your house away from this fucking awful city."

CHAPTER EIGHTEEN

Feet on the sofa, cup on the floor, Hazel was reading when Diana burst through the door on New Year's Eve.

"Get your fucking feet down," she barked as she crossed the room to the drinks cart.

"You're back early," Hazel said, planting her feet.

"Back early? What would I do without your utterly brilliant observations, Hazel?" Diana picked up the vodka, contemplated a glass for a moment before taking a deep swallow straight from the bottle. "I think you have the right idea, Hazel, not going with men."

"It wasn't my idea," she whispered.

"What?"

"It wasn't an idea I had one day. It's who I am."

Diana took another deep draught, head tilted back, so she was looking down her nose at Hazel.

"Does it fucking matter either way?" she muttered, once sated. She took another drink, gave the now empty bottle a shake. "Elsbeth! Elsbeth!" She turned to Hazel. "Is she here?"

"The woman's goddamn ancient. Give her a chance."

"Never mind, me and you are going to have our own party tonight. I don't need anyone but you right now." She replaced the empty vodka with gin.

"Can you believe that bastard? Dropping me? I was a star long before him and I'll be one long after he's gone."

She took another drink. Hazel wondered how she could still stand after consuming so much in such a small amount of time.

"What was I saying?" Diana said, slightly swaying now. "Ah, yes. We—we are going to have our own party."

"I think you ought to go to bed."

"Nonsense." Diana stumbled through the room, clutching the bottle as though it was a lifeline that could be snatched away from her at any moment. Hazel got up and followed her, ready to catch her should she fall. After a few false starts, and some bashing into furniture resulting in a smashed vase, Diana made it to what Hazel thought of as the museum. She hadn't been in the room since that day with Elsbeth, but her thoughts had often returned to it. Hazel had been apprehensive about Diana's ability to navigate the crowded room, yet she managed it with surprising ease. Reaching the back of the room revealed a door. Diana opened it, promptly falling through it to reveal a screening room. Plush sofas, another well-stocked bar.

"Sit down." She gestured to one of the sofas. "I'm going to show you what a true great looks like." She stumbled over to the projector at the back of the room and, with surprisingly swift competence, laced on a reel. The screen flicked to life.

Hazel had watched silent pictures as a young girl with her father but they'd always had the organ accompany them. True silence, save for the slight whirl and click of the projector, made it all so much eerier. Diana sat beside Hazel. The pictures were of course Mae's. Spliced, so they ran one after another.

The first couple were standard fare, then suddenly the room was bathed in a blue glow. Diana must have seen Hazel's wonder at this.

"Tinted, it's a trick to give the sense of it being nighttime. Keep watching. There's more of that to come."

This was no lie. Hazel watched scenes of lavender, red, green, and amber play as Diana explained the significance of each colour.

When Hazel turned to Diana, her eyes were wet with tears.

"Everything I have is because of her. I remember when we shot this scene." A lilting laugh. "I thought I was going to die. There was no safety harness—" She stopped abruptly, looking at Hazel with a glint of suspicion, as though she had coxed the words from her.

Hazel stared back at her; bathed in a lavender glow, Diana's eyes seemed impossibly wide. The reel ran out, plunging the room back to semi-darkness.

"Who are you?" Hazel's voice held a note of fear. "What are you?"

In the low light, Diane's face was not her own, not fully. Behind the floating mask was another face. Mae's. Then, in an instance, it was gone.

"I'm whoever I want to be."

***

When Hazel opened her eyes, her first thought was that she was dreaming. Even in the dark, she instantly knew that it was Diana's bed she was in.

But why and how?

She remembered being in the screening room watching the old Mae pictures. She remembered Diana getting upset when she tried to leave. The way Diana clung to her after the empty gin bottle had shattered against the wall, flung by Diana.

Then the kiss, full of anger and possessiveness. The pain as fingers entwined in her hair, pulling Hazel's head back so she was looking up at Diana.

After that, nothing.

She was still fully clothed, although that wasn't any indicator that nothing further had happened between them. Diana was on her side at the far edge of the bed, still clothed, her breathing so shallow that for a moment Hazel wasn't entirely sure she was breathing at all. Hazel instinctively brushed her thumb across her fingertips, finding no evidence she had touched Diana. A mixture of disappointment and relief swept through her. Disappointment that yet again she had come so close to finally having her again, relief it hadn't occurred while she was blacked out.

It seemed to be happening more and more lately, great swaths of time she couldn't remember anything about. Hazel had put it down to drink at first. She had very rarely drank before she meeting Diana, but she'd had nothing stronger than tea last night.

Was this an early sign of madness? The vast majority of people would argue that she was already ready for the asylum because of her "perversion."

Hazel, moving as slowly as possible in order not to wake Diana, tried to get off the bed.

"No, stay," Diana slurred, capturing Hazel's wrist and pulling her back down. She shifted, nuzzling into the crook of Hazel's neck, long limbs draped over her, pinning her down so there was no escape. Hazel felt the hitching of Diana's breath and dampness spreading at her collar. Obviously, not enough time had passed in which to sober up.

"Do you know what it's like to be cast aside? I used to be someone to so many people. I never had trouble keeping a man or getting any role I wanted. I want to say that a woman reaches a certain age and they're done. But this body is younger than Crawford and Hepburn; they keep getting cast. It's a cruel game. This business and the rules are different for everyone."

"Why do you want to play it so badly?" Hazel rubbed Diana's back gently. "You've enough money to last you the rest of your life. Why not just enjoy it?"

"What, sit and rot like that mad woman with her chimp over on Sunset?" Diana's back muscles tightened, her taut and stiff body radiating rage, "I could have chosen anyone of a dozen girls like you out the gutter, but I thought you understood what it's like to be cast aside, unloved, unwanted."

Hazel had crossed an ocean for that reason. "I wish I'd never met you."

"You're free to leave, but you won't."

There was nothing else to be said after this. The only sound was Diana's sobs fading into soft snores.

Chapter Nineteen

It had taken some wheedling of Elsbeth to find out where Quinn was, and after that, a performance that would have made Diana proud to get past the nurse at the reception desk. What Hazel had thought to be a pretty accurate approximation of Quinn's East Coast accent had served to convince that she was Quinn's sister, come to visit.

True to her word Diana had spared no expense in ensuring Quinn had the very best care. Quinn's private room was light and airy, decked out in blonde wood and pastel fabrics. She was sat in a plush armchair, nose in a book, the first time Hazel had ever seen her reading. She tapped on the open door to get Quinn's attention.

She looked up, face alight. "Hazel!"

Before Hazel knew what had happened, she had been enveloped in a hug followed by a slap across the face.

"That woman better not be with you," Quinn hissed so none of the orderlies in the hall would hear.

"Quinn, I'm so sorry, I should have come sooner."

Quinn went to the doorway and looked out into the hall.

"She's not with me."

Quinn settled back into the chair. "Why are you here?"

"I—I need to know what happened that night. Do you remember?"

"Yes."

"And?"

"And what? If I'd kept my mouth shut, they might've let me go after a week. I'm not going to risk them thinking I've not made any progress."

"Quinn, please." Hazel was on her knees in front of Quinn. "No one else need know, but I have to."

"Hey!" A sharp rap on the door punctuated the word. Hazel turned around. A male orderly stood at the door regarding them both with suspicion. "We'll have none of that here."

Under his watchful eye, Hazel stood and moved a respectable distance away from Quinn. "That's better," he said, before carrying on down the hallway.

"Diana did *something* to me," Quinn whispered.

Hazel's mind instantly went back to that day in Francis's office. "Did she—did she touch you?"

"No. I remember after you fell asleep, Diana asked if I wanted to see the rest of the house. I said yes, so she showed me around. It was all your typical rich person's bullshit, but then we went into this room that's like a shrine. I can't remember who, but they were big in silent pictures. It was really weird how she spoke about this woman …"

"Go on."

"So, after she was done showing me some dresses and props, she takes me into this other room, which was like a little movie theatre. I was thinking, God no, I do not want to be watching silent pictures with this woman! But she pours me another drink, and that couch was just so comfortable. She puts the film on and she just starts droning on and on, and by this point I'm feeling pretty tired, so I closed my eyes and drifted off.

I don't know how long I'd been dozing but when I woke up the film had ended and Diana was staring at me.

Except it wasn't her—" Quinn stared at a point behind Hazel.

"Quinn?" Hazel turned around.

The orderly from earlier was at the door again, his hand on the frame. Hazel stared at him a moment until, seemingly bored, he went back to his rounds.

"Hazel, I can't do this." Quinn swallowed, hard. "I can't go down this road again. I need to concentrate on getting better."

"I'm sorry, I should leave."

"No, you can stay. I just want to talk about nice, normal things though. Can we do that?"

"Yes, we can do that."

***

Quinn's words gnawed at the back of her mind. Hadn't she sat in the darkness and looked upon that terrible visage, or was Quinn's alleged memory creeping into her own hazy recollection? She thought back to her school days, to dares of calling upon Bloody Mary in darkened rooms. Once, her and her friends had been convinced that they had succeeded, running screaming outside into the safety of daylight.

Only they hadn't, had they?

The play of light and shadow can easily trick the eyes.

It would be a perfectly reasonable explanation that tired eyes would, having been forced to watch the silver screen for hours on end, project a ghostly image of their own, overlaying Mae's face over that of Diana's.

Diana was her own special brand of wickedness, but it was one truly entwined with and born of this city.

***

Diana was on the telephone when Hazel got home, draped casually on the chaise longue in the hallway, rose-tipped cigarette almost burnt down to the filter in the ashtray balanced on one thigh. Seeing Hazel, she snapped her fingers and pointed towards the silver case by the telephone.

"That's wonderful …" She took the cigarette from Hazel, putting it in her mouth before raising her eyebrows in a *haven't you forgotten* something gesture. Hazel picked up the lighter, leaning forward to reach Diana.

She took a deep drag of the now lit cigarette. "Simply wonderful, darling, we'll speak soon."

She hung up the phone without uttering a goodbye.

"Well, once again, Hazel, I've pulled us back from the brink."

"Wonderful," Hazel muttered.

"We're going freelance. It's the future, darling. The days of being tied to just one studio are coming to an end."

Chapter Twenty

It's a women's picture, Diana told Hazel, the kind that made her.

"You'll be playing my daughter." She took a gulp of gin before her lips settled into a sullen line, no doubt thinking of when she played the daughters, the love interests.

Hazel thought of how embarrassing it'd be to call the woman who, despite herself, she still aches for with every fibre of her being, *'Mom.'*

"At least you'll be able to see a master at work, Hazel. Learn how it's done and maybe this one won't be a flop."

Hazel nodded affably, too tired to argue.

***

A month later, and they were on set, ready to film *Edith Wright* with Tom Herjervak directing.

Diana, being the big name, had her own private dressing room which Hazel nervously waited outside of. Something or someone had enraged Diana, Hazel recognised the icy tone of her voice masking the white hot rage beneath.

The door was suddenly flung open and a redheaded woman strode out, almost knocking Hazel over.

"Kat?"

Kat's eyes flashed in confusion.

She's wondering how I know her name.

"Tom told me who you are. Remember, we met on—"

"Yes, I remember. It was a shame what happened to Olivia, and it was a shame for you. Tom showed me the footage. You would have been great."

"Thank you." It was only then that she noticed the wet gleam in Kat's eyes. Hazel put a hand on her shoulder and steered her away from the dressing room door.

"Diana," she began. "Diana can be—"

"An evil and unreasonable bitch?"

Hazel looked down.

"She's not the first to take out their frustrations on me and she won't be the last." Kat sighed. "The costumes aren't as glamorous as she'd hoped. But she's not the twenty-something shop girl anymore. Sooner she realises that, the better. After all, the woman is literally old enough to play your mother."

A few months ago Hazel would have jumped to Diana's defence. Argued that she had earned respect. But the glow that had always surrounded Diana was fading for Hazel ever since she'd visited Quinn.

She'd received a letter from Quinn that morning. She'd been released and travelled straight to her sisters in New York. The letter had been an invitation as well.

Maybe she should go out to New York, Hazel thought. She could try theatre.

She'd be free from the scrutiny of Diana and the industry. Maybe she could even find someone.

"I said, would you like to get a malt at Schwab's with me, Hazel?"

She looked at Kat, the red hair and brown eyes. Hers were a softer beauty than Diana's, warmth radiating from her. Kat glanced about before taking Hazel's hand, her thumb moving in slow, deliberate circles on her palm.

"So." Kat's eyes never left Hazel's. "Would you like to go?" Kat continued to make those featherlight circles on her palm.

"Yes—yes! Please."

Kat let Hazel's hand drop.

"I'll see you later then."

Kat walked over to talk to Tom, a knowing smile on his face.

The euphoria Hazel felt died when she noticed Diana standing in the doorway of her dressing room, staring at the back of Kat's head with a hatred so palpable and fierce it made Hazel shudder.

***

Hazel felt more alive in the half hour she spent with Kat sat at Schwab's counter then she'd had for months.

It was a half hour of subtle touches, of them carefully gauging the other's every reaction.

She likes me, I think?

But a women couldn't simply can't say to another woman, "I'm attracted to you." No, that was far too dangerous. You had to play the game.

Hazel had forgotten the thrill of it. Diana had extracted her feelings from her in a matter of hours and used them against her ever since.

Diana had been silent on the drive home from the studio. Hazel spent the short journey rehearsing in her mind what she was going to tell Diana.

I appreciate all you've done for me …

I just think it's time I moved on …

Hazel rushed into the house, Diana a few steps behind. Hazel's heart was beating wild, and she turned around just as the door clicked shut.

"Diana, I—"

Diana closed the gap between them, grabbed Hazel by the waist and kissed her.

Hazel quivered as Diana's hands moved up her back and then buried themselves in her hair. Gone were the painful, spiteful tugs that had marked their prior kisses. Instead, Diana's hands gently guided Hazel.

After a moment, she broke away, her hands dropping to Hazel's shoulders and holding them firmly. "Take me to bed."

"What?"

"No questions, Hazel. No words, just show me that you still want me." She brushed her thumb across Hazel's bottom lip before turning away. Hazel watched the deliberate roll of her hips as she climbed the stairs.

Diana paused halfway up and, without looking back, she said, "Are you coming?"

***

Diana reclined on her bed.

"Strip." The command sent waves of arousal through Hazel. She undressed slowly, revelling in the look of hunger that filled Diana's eyes. Once naked, Diana bid Hazel to lie next to her.

"This body belongs to me," she said, her hand hovering above Hazel's thigh, so achingly close Hazel could feel the heat from Diana's palm.

"Tell me this body belongs to me."

"I'm yours," Hazel breathed.

"That's not what I asked you to say."

"This body belongs to you."

"Good girl." She moved her hand along Hazel, past her hip, before settling on her lower stomach.

She'd never been so wet, her arousal almost painful. Hazel shifted, desperate for any kind of contact. Diana laughed.

It would be just like Diana to get her to this point, then deny her release.

"What to do about you, Hazel? I didn't mind you going with my double."

Hazel stilled.

"Oh yes, I know you went back for more. But this little redhead in costuming? We can't be having that." She reached over Hazel for the cigarette case on the bedside cabinet. Hazel tried to sit up.

"No, don't move." Diana lit the cigarette and took a deep drag, blowing the hot smoke into Hazel's face. "I've hardly touched you and look at yourself. Do you honestly think that girl could make you feel this way?"

Hazel opened her eyes and looked at herself in the mirror above Diana's bed, writhing beneath Diana's non-existent touch.

You're ruined.

She's ruined you.

And you crave it.

"Tell me what you need, Hazel."

"You," Hazel whined.

"You already have me. I'm right here."

"I want—I need you to touch me."

"Tell me more."

"I need you to fuck me."

"And if I do?"

"Yes?"

"You'll forget all about this silly notion about going to New York?"

"How did you—"

"Elsbeth told me about that letter from Quinn."

"I won't leave, I promise. Diana, please!"

Diana clumsily plunged two fingers in; Hazel winced in pain as Diana inexpertly and violently thrusted.

Hazel had been so close to the edge that, despite the pain, she tumbled over in less than a minute. Diana stayed inside her until the last shudder had passed before withdrawing. The look of disgust as she examined her fingers killed the peaceful bliss that had always followed climax.

Hazel reached for Diana.

"I'm going downstairs for a drink. Clean yourself up and get to bed. I want you fresh for tomorrow."

CHAPTER TWENTY-ONE

"I had a really nice time yesterday."

Hazel had successfully avoided Kat all day, certain she'd take one look at her and see the shame clinging to her.

Fucking pathetic.

"I thought maybe we could go somewhere more private. Say, my apartment?" Kat smiled shyly, her hand going to the back of her neck as she looked down at her feet.

So goddamn adorable. "Kat …"

"Yes?"

"I think you may have the wrong idea about me." A look of horror passed over Kat's face.

"I'm so sorry, I didn't mean to offend you—"

"No, no, you're right about—I'm—I like …"

There was no need to finish. Kat nodded solemnly.

"You just don't like me?"

"I do, it's just not the right time"

"Because of Diana? Tom told me you've a weird fixation on her."

"Don't you dare judge us."

"'Us'? You're together?"

Hazel chewed at her cheek. What exactly did last night mean? True, there'd been a certain amount of loathing, Hazel had been with women before who couldn't let go of the shame of desiring another woman. But Diana had said in no uncertain terms that Hazel belonged to her.

"I wish you'd told me before I made an idiot of myself." Kat smiled. "There's no reason we couldn't be friends though. Having someone who understands exactly who you really are, someone who won't judge you. It's more important than you think. You'll go crazy in this town without someone like that."

"I'd like that."

"Like what?" Diana asked, then, without waiting for an answer, "Hazel, are you riding home with me? Or …" She looked at Kat, not bothering to try and hide the sneer on her face. "Have you made other arrangements?"

"I'll see you around, Hazel," Kat said, before walking away.

"It's good for your image to be friendly with the crew, but …" Diana plucked a long red hair from Hazel's shoulder, "you don't have to be that friendly."

Hazel's heart raced. "We weren't—"

"Girl sheds like a cat."

***

It was late when Hazel knocked on Diana's door, cursing herself even as she did. When they had arrived home, Hazel embraced Diana, only to be pushed away. "God, you're needy," she'd said as she kicked off her heels. "Get me a drink and I'll see how I feel later."

Hazel knocked again. "Fine, come on in."

Diana sat on the bed, surrounded by paper. "Terrible," she muttered.

As Hazel drew closer she saw it was pages of the *Edith Wright* screenplay all annotated with Diana's spidery hand.

Hazel moved a stack of sheets and sat down on the edge of the bed.

"What is it?" Diana said, her gaze never lifting from the paper.

"I thought we could spend some time together."

"We're together every day."

"Time on set doesn't really count. I know we can't go out in public like you did with Raymond, but that doesn't mean we can't do other things as a couple."

"You're worse than Raymond wanting to paw me all the time. And we're not a couple, nor will we ever be."

"What are we then?"

"Petulance doesn't suit you." Diana picked up a page, brandishing it. "Always strive to be better, Hazel. Like this, this is not good enough."

"Why did you say yes to it then?"

"Tom will be thrilled with my suggestions," she said, ignoring Hazel.

"It was your suggestions that ruined his last picture."

My picture.

"If you'd have been committed to the role …"

Hazel kissed Diana. "I don't want to talk about that," she said, before recapturing Diana's lips. Diana's hand went to Hazel's neck before sliding down, her palm resting against her breastbone. Hazel's heart raced in anticipation of where Diana's hand would go next.

"Hazel?" she whispered.

"Yes," Hazel whimpered.

"What the fuck do you think you're doing?" She pushed hard, sending Hazel to the floor.

"Let me make one thing clear, this"—she gestured—"all of this I am in control of. I will decide when and if you can kiss me. And don't just sit there looking like an idiot with your mouth wide open. Make yourself useful and tidy this up."

Hazel got up from the floor, the sting of Diana's rejection surpassing that of the pain at the base of her back. She gathered the loose papers into a stack and placed them on the side table.

"Sit down." Diana's tone was softer now. "You must understand that after lifetimes of having men trying to control me, I find it difficult to give up control."

"It's not about controlling one another, at least that's not how it's ever been for me."

Diana scoffed. "Hazel, don't you understand that control is all it ever boils down to? You either have control over others or they have it over you. No inbetween."

She's right, Quinn's voice said. *She controls every part of you. And you love it, it excites you.*

Diana slid a hand into Hazel's hair, grasping tightly. Hazel moaned.

See, you love it when she's rough with you.

"Make yourself useful and tell Elsbeth I want her. I'll let you know when I'm ready for you."

CHAPTER TWENTY-TWO

Hazel watched the way Tom's jaw clenched as Diana showed him the revised pages. After a moment of Diana gesticulating wildly, the pages flew into the air and Diana stormed off to her dressing room.

"Are you okay?" Hazel tentatively asked as Tom bent down to gather the pages.

"I'm fine, which is more than I can say about Kat. She'll never tell you herself but you really hurt her yesterday."

"I—"

"This thing you have with Diana—"

"I wish people would mind their own business about that. Plus you can't dislike her that much. You fought for her, after all."

"I fought for you, Hazel. Diana came as part of the deal, your deal."

"I …" It had never occurred to Hazel that Tom, that anyone, would fight for her.

"You have so much potential, it's raw, but it's there. If you cared about your career or yourself, ditch Diana."

***

The following weeks passed in a blur for Hazel. She saw Kat a few times around the set but apart from the occasional nod and hello had no interaction with her. Tom had cooled towards her as well, no longer the pillar of warmth she could lean upon. It was her own fault, she knew. Her refusal to let go of Diana had cemented her isolation.

No Quinn, that first letter had been her last. Though what did she expect? She hadn't written Quinn back.

Diana, although displeased with Tom's refusal to give in to her suggested changes, was pleased with the first previews.

In high spirits at the thought of her grand comeback, she had invited Hazel to her bed a few nights. It was different to that first night. Diana hardly touched her. That didn't bother Hazel. Every touch of Diana's body sent shock-waves through her. The only time she felt truly alive now was when she was close to Diana. When forced apart she felt sick, hungover; her body craved this woman. At the back of her mind Hazel knew she should be terrified at this, between that and her increasing periods of lost time.

But when she looked at Diana beneath her, her hips moving to meet Hazel's every movement of her hand, that all disappeared.

***

It wasn't long until Hazel was picked up for another picture. *Edith Wright* was a resounding success, and keen to capitalise on that success they once again paired Hazel with Tom directing.

A comedy with a straight-talking Connecticut Yankee as her co-star.

Hazel took an immediate liking to her.

Beneath the air of haughtiness was someone who, much like Kat—Hazel felt a stab of pain at the remembrance—was thoroughly unimpressed with the idea of being a star. There for the pure joy of the craft, a woman who eschewed Los Angeles, preferring her own family home and only coming to Hollywood to film, after which she'd be on the first plane back to where she could take walks along the rocky coast with the pack of dogs she shared her home with, play tennis, and golf.

She'd sit crocheting between takes. So unlike Diana, who veered wildly between screaming at crew members one moment and giving out small gifts whilst empathically saying their names in order to prove that she did, in fact, know them and was just a normal everyday woman who just happened to be a star.

"How you doing, kid?" Celia said, putting down the needles and patting the space next to her for Hazel to sit down.

"Good, thank you." Hazel remained standing, Diana had an unerring habit of knowing when she started to get friendly with people, more specifically women who Diana saw as a threat.

"You gonna stand there all day?" Celia picked up the needles again.

Celia was no threat, though she reminded Hazel of a friend her mother had once had, a woman who had shown her more maternal affection in the short time she'd known her then Hazel's own mother had her entire life.

"A lot of the women I've worked with over the years see their co-stars as rivals. Not me, I guess maybe because I was never what you'd call an It Girl." She eyed Hazel. "You don't have to be afraid of me, although I understand why you might be, having worked with some of the top tier bitches you have."

Celia carried on. "I've worked with Diana a few times, we came up together. She seemed such a sweet girl back then, so naive, she could not do enough for you."

Hazel's mind drifted, she didn't want to hear more unkind words about Diana.

"All set to marry her high school sweetheart. Sure there were rumours that she slept around, but so what if she was. Then something changed when Mae took an interest in her."

Hazel snapped back at the mention of Mae. "Mae? As in Mae Joseph?"

"I'd have thought you were too young to know about her. But yes, it was the strangest thing. She showed absolutely no signs of having any talent. Mae, being one of the few greats that made the transition to sound, could have had a few more years if she hadn't killed herself."

"Mae committed suicide?"

"It was kept out of all the papers, naturally. She couldn't stand to fade away. She left Diana everything, her house, money, even that German maid of hers. And somehow, she left her Goddamn talent to her as well. I don't know if it was being financially secure, but Diana got bolder. She ditched the husband, took a new surname and became a force of nature. She started playing the men of this town like Goddamn violins."

"What do you mean by that?"

"All of a sudden she knew things about everyone. Mae must have told her all her secrets before she died, her or the maid. She modelled herself after Mae, people who'd known Mae from the silent days used to comment on how alike they were. They used to joke that the ghost of Mae possessed Diana."

Hazel felt as if a tennis ball had lodged in her throat, painfully dry. She knew Celia's words had been said in jest, but they explained so much. The way Elsbeth sometimes spoke as though Diana and Mae were one person. Diana's own reverence of Mae, the way she spoke of events as if she were there and not merely giving a secondhand account of them.

"You look positively ill!"

"I—really don't—"

Hazel lent forward, head between her knees. It couldn't possibly be true, it didn't make sense.

It makes perfect sense.

"Are you going to be sick?"

Hazel raised her hand. "I just need a moment. I'll be fine. I just need—" The bile which spilled out of her stomach was bitter and dark, the only thing that had passed her lips was black coffee. It was splattered all over Celia's white shoes. Tears pricked at Hazel's eyes, all at once she felt as though she was a young child as she braced herself for Celia's anger.

"I'm so sorry, your—"

"If you think this is the worst thing I've ever had on my feet. My girl, I've horses, dogs—it's a goddamn menagerie at my house."

"Thank you," Hazel whispered.

"You've nothing to worry about here, we'll get this cleared up and you can take a nap. I'll talk to Tom, I'm sure we could work around your absence for the rest of the day."

"Thank you so much," Hazel repeated, the tears in full flow now. "I think I'd like to just go straight home though."

"I'm sure I could arrange that."

***

Hazel had gone straight up to her bedroom, avoiding Diana who, at this time of day, would be soaking up the sun by the pool.

Her stomach had calmed since that initial shock. This was why she was here; Diana saw her as nothing more than a replacement.

The obsession with turning her into the star was nothing to do with love or affection; it was to secure Diana's, or should that be Mae's, own future in this town. She had to get out of this house, away from her. The urge to go to Laura reared, bringing with it the memory Diana's touches. How they'd always coincided with Hazel's periods of self-doubt. Always just enough to keep her hanging on. She must have thought she'd hit the jackpot when she'd found her, no family to notice the change in her that would come, so desperate in her need for her that she could be manipulated to do anything.

She could check into a hotel under a false name, disappear for a while until she figured out what to do next. But there was Kat.

Sweet, kind, beautiful Kat, who had shown genuine interest in her. More than that, Hazel needed to talk about it, even if only to be told it was all crazy, that it couldn't possibly be true. The damage Diana had done to her was real and she could only hope Kat would forgive her for being such a blind idiot.

She went to the wardrobe and started filling a case, making no effort at neatness.

"Hazel?" Elsbeth was at the door. "You are home early."

"I don't feel well."

"I'll get Miss Diana, she can call a doctor for you."

Hazel thought back to Quinn being dragged out by the men in white coats. Would Diana do that to her? No. Because by doing that she'd be risking her own future reputation, she'd worked hard to keep Hazel scandal free.

"It's not so serious as that, I think it's down to something I ate."

Elsbeth eyed her with suspicion. *Maybe,* Hazel thought, *she wasn't a good actress after all.*

"Please don't tell Diana, I don't want her to worry."

"And the clothes?"

Hazel looked down at the bundle of clothes she held tight to her chest. "I'm rearranging?" She cursed at the way her voice had risen, turning what should have been a statement into a question. "I'm rearranging," she asserted.

To prove the point, she dropped the bundle onto the bed and started to arrange by type into piles. She felt Elsbeth's eyes on the back of her as she worked. There would be no chance of leaving with any of her possessions. After what seemed like an age to Hazel, she heard the thump of Elsbeth's heavy shoes as she went down the hallway and back downstairs to Diana.

Hazel finished carefully putting away everything. Should Diana come to check she'd need to be able to show her work.

There was no way she'd be able to leave tonight without rousing Diana's suspicions. The best course of action would be to go downstairs and sit by the pool, to fawn over Diana as she let the sun seep into her long legs. To let her ask Hazel to put oil on her, to let her laugh at the way she'd become flustered when faced with that expanse of smooth skin.

She took a cool shower, changed into something lighter for the pool and went to face Diana.

CHAPTER TWENTY-THREE

That evening, once the sun had passed over and it grew cool, they moved to the lounge. Diana began the familiar ritual of fixing drinks. Hazel sat, her eyes growing heavy. *I'll just close them a moment.*

The clink of ice against crystal startled her. Glancing out the window, she saw it was full dark, and in her grogginess thought how she missed seeing stars.

Real ones.

There was always a light burning somewhere in this city, obscuring them.

It made her heart ache.

Take your money and go home.

She closed her eyes again, felt the weight of Diana sitting next to her, the fragrance of her perfume mixed with the suntan oil.

"Drink."

Diana put the cool glass into her hand.

"What is it?" Hazel asked, surprised to find her words were already slurred.

Had she been drinking already? Was she that drunk she'd forgotten?

"Something to relax you," Diana said.

"I—I was already."

"I need you to tell me what Celia said to you today."

"Nothing."

"Nothing?"

"She—she told me about her animals."

"And that caused you to try to pack your bags and run away, did it? Oh Hazel, I think we can do better than that? What did she tell you?"

The hand gently caressing her thigh now grasped tighter, digging her nails in.

Hazel gasped at the mixture of pleasure and pain that ran through her.

"She told me how Mae left all her money and property to you and about that joke, about how her ghost must have possessed you because you became so much like her."

Diana's eyes darkened.

"I know that's not true though, about you being possessed."

"Why would you feel the need to say you don't believe what is clearly a ridiculous notion? You really don't do yourself any favours sometimes, Hazel. Refuting something like that shows that you must have considered it being true."

"Does it?" Hazel asked, confused.

"Yes, you don't want people to think you're an idiot, do you?"

"No."

"Oh, you sweet, simple girl. So beautiful, so much potential." She leant forward and kissed Hazel. "If only you'd give in to me."

Hazel returned the kiss..

CHAPTER TWENTY-FOUR

October 5th '98

David's father has died and with his death comes the revelation that he had sold the 1000 acres David was set to inherit, the money's all gone as well. The house that we live in.

All that's left is the smallholding. It's been empty since before the war.

The floorboards are rotted, the roof leaks. He says that he can till the land, that it must be good soil as it's laid fallow for so long, when I said he doesn't know the first thing about working the land, his father's labourers did all that, he punched me so hard in the stomach I vomited. It seeped into the floor cracks. We will smell it for months.

At least he never hits my face.

Even when my body has been broken, my skin shades of yellow and purple he's always sure to tell me how perfect my face is.

What will he do to me when time takes its toll and it's no longer perfect?

March 10th '99

The woods to the rear of the property scare me. I hear noises late at night they don't stop until the early morning.

David tells me I must sleep, that all our strength would be needed for planting season.

Nothing will grow here.

The earth is dead. and so will I be if I don't get out of here.

Sept 4th '99

I often hear the thing in the woods speaking to me.

Whispers late at night. Telling me that I could be free of this place, free of him.

If only I took control.

December 31st '99

I went out into the woods, barefoot into the night, to speak with that which lives in the woods. I have no name for it, and when I asked it would not give me one. I listened as it told me what it could do for me. The power I could have. I asked what it would want in return.

Nothing, it said. I've been watching you from afar. I see the pain, this is an offer of help. All you have to do is take control.

David beat me harder than he ever has before, every inch of my body is bloody and blacked.

As I stared up at the ceiling, he thrusted and grunted.

I thought, this is a new century about to dawn and I WILL take control of it.

Chapter Twenty-Five

It was chaos when Hazel arrived on set.

"We tried to contact you," Tom said, his hand grasping at his hair. His eyes unfocused.

"What happened?"

"A lighting rig fell."

"Oh my God, was anyone hurt?

"Celia's dead."

"What?"

"It was quick—"

Hazel looked at the blood splatter on his shirt, his left cheek.

"I was mapping out the scene with her … I felt it, the air move, as it fell. But I didn't know it was a light. Not until I felt something warm on my cheek and I looked to Celia and she was there, on the floor …"

A thought came to Hazel. "Tom?"

He lifted his gaze to meet Hazel's, but didn't really focus on her.

His eyes still held that faraway look.

"Did—have you seen Diana on the set today?"

"Yes. She came by looking for Kat, of all people." His eyes darted around. "I wonder where she is."

"Who, Diana?"

"No, Kat. I haven't seen her for hours."

"I have to go," Hazel said.

"Yeah, we won't be shooting anything today. Hazel, with what happened with Olivia and now Celia, I'm done in this town. It's like I'm fucking cursed."

Not you, Hazel thought. *Me.*

***

Hazel had never moved as fast in her life as she did now. Francis, Olivia and now Celia: the common thread in all of them was Diana. She was always at the scene.

And everything in her told her that she'd taken Kat, for what purpose she didn't know. She burst through the door to find Elsbeth waiting for her in the foyer.

"Miss Diana is expecting you."

"Does she have Kat?"

Elsbeth looked puzzled. "Miss Diana does not have a cat, she despises pets."

"The girl!"

"Yes, she has a girl."

Hazel raced past. Although Elsbeth had not said where Diana was waiting, instinct told her they'd be in the Mae room.

She made her way through the clutter to the screening room. Kat was there, seemingly sleeping on the sofa, but no sign of Diana. Hazel went to her, placing her hand to Kat's neck. Her pulse was steady and her breathing deep, but she could not be woken.

"She's for you." Diana stood in a doorway Hazel had never seen before, ringed by smoke. "Or at least the part of you that will remain. Elsbeth isn't getting younger and I can't be without her." She crossed over to the sofa and caressed Kat's face. "I'm not sure if it'll work. I've only ever done this for myself."

"Done what?" Hazel asked shakily.

Diana straightened. "Let me show you something. Don't worry, your little friend is quite safe."

Hazel followed Diana to the previously unknown room.

"You had your suspicions of me before and Celia confirmed them, didn't she?"

"You didn't have to kill her."

"You're right, I didn't, but she vexed me. She might have caused you to run away. I wasn't planning on doing this quite so soon but as I said, I can't risk you running. I want you to see with your own eyes the real me."

On a pedestal stood a wax figure of Mae. Hazel had visited waxworks before but never had she seen this level of detail. She looked as though she could spring to life at any moment.

"I was exquisite, wasn't I?" Diana said with a sigh.

"You're mad, absolutely mad."

"I found Diana much like I did you. Both of you hungry and desperate. Although Diana was attracted to fame whilst your fixation was with me. It made you both so easy to control though, pathetic in your own ways. I can still hear her, a little niggle, at the back of my mind. Don't worry though, I'll be leaving her behind. After all, two's company, three's a crowd."

So struck by the beauty of Mae and the horror of her words, Hazel didn't realise that Diana was by her side.

"There's another room that adjoins this one, Diana deserves her own memorial after all. Might need a bigger pedestal. It's all in your name now, the house, the money. I think a plane crash will be a fitting end to Diana. One where the body won't be found. It was such a bother to steal my old one from the coroners. I'd rather not risk doing that again."

"You mean …" Hazel swallowed. "That's really her? You?"

"I couldn't have her made her into ash or left to rot beneath the ground. Perfect beauty made immortal."

"You're fucking crazy, this can't be true. You're not really her, you're just a bitch with an obsession."

Hazel turned; she and Kat were getting out of this house even if she had to carry her. Diana was not prepared to relinquish her; she grabbed Hazel's wrist, pulling her towards her. Hazel pulled back and Diana's hand slipped, sending Hazel careering backwards into Mae. The waxwork hit the ground, splitting open the figure's cheek.

Beneath the wax was pale, necrotic flesh.

Hazel screamed, then all went black.

CHAPTER TWENTY-SIX

Photoplay Magazine

March 1974

Hazel Sumner displays the effortless charm that comes with having nothing left to prove. Her rise in popularity during the war years was meteoric. The English Rose who became America's sweetheart.

Never married but linked to many of Hollywood's most dashing leading men, she, unlike so many of her contemporaries, has stayed relevant. Making the move into television …

The young woman turned off the cassette recorder.

"Can we go off the record?" Her excitement raised her voice an octave. "I don't normally gush over the people I interview, but when I was told I had you for this assignment … well, I—I watched so many of your films on TV when I was a little girl." A nervous laugh. "I'm sorry, you must get this all the time."

A woman with burnt auburn hair that must have once been bright red set a tray with a pitcher of lemonade down on the table beside them. Hazel thanked the woman, who gave a brief nod of her head before going back inside.

"I'm glad my pictures have reached the younger generation." Hazel's accent had lost the mid-Atlantic clipped tone of the pictures of the mid-forties, replaced by a generic West coast accent.

"This is going to sound so silly, but I used to dream of being you."

Hazel reached across the table, picked up a silver cigarette case and took out a cigarette with a rose-petal tip.

"This may sound silly, but what if I told you I could make that dream come true?"

Acknowledgements

I'd like to thank Kelly White, Shauna Mc Eleney and Vivian Kasley for reading and providing feedback on the first draft.

Rae Knowles for being my champion and a wonderful creative partner.

Heather and Steve at Brigids Gate for taking a chance on me.

And Daniella Batsheva for her beautiful cover illustration.

ABOUT THE AUTHOR

April Yates is an English writer of dark and queer fiction. Her other longer work includes the novella, *Ashthorne*, published by Ghost Orchid Press and the novel, *Lies That Bind* (co-authored with Rae Knowles), due for release via Brigids Gate in 2024.

Find her at https://aprilyates.com/.

CONTENT WARNINGS

Eye trauma
Mentions of sexual assault and attempted rape
Forcible removal of teeth

MORE FROM BRIGIDS GATE PRESS

Caleb Jenkins is a bullied middle schooler that everyone calls Clay Boy, due to the way he uses clay therapy to cope with the tragic murder of his mother at the hands of a serial killer. While at school, he discovers a playful video on how to create an imaginary best friend called a tulpa, but the more he interacts with his mental creation the more real and self-thinking it becomes, eventually convincing Caleb to sculpt a body for it to inhabit in order to unleash the hate that both share upon his bullies and the entire community of Wheeler's Cove, Tennessee.

The story of a girl begins with a boy. On Christmas morning, 1982, nine-year-old Jude Bendz survives the shocking and mysterious death of his twin sister, Mary. Bewildered by grief, he is comforted when, miraculously, Mary's ghost appears, her spirit quickly informing a series of fantastic apparitions through which her life—and death—come into clearer focus. Problems soon arise, however, when his sister, promising salvation, places him at the center of a wide, yet narrowing plot that increasingly puts his life in mortal danger.

A novel that transcends its historical moment, *Being Dead* brilliantly subverts the conventions of the traditional Ghost story. Reconstructing her own death through a series of spooky visitations and cryptic clues that, in time, seem to assume the shape of formal challenges, Mary creates for Jude a blueprint that blurs the line between truth and revenge, love and hate, an account that threatens to shatter their family's perfect image.

Luminous, evocative, and set amidst the decline of American exceptionalism and the nuclear family, this is at once an enthralling adventure, a stirring love story, and a work of striking power in the face of stark solitude. As Mary interweaves elements of a set past that portends a harrowing future, life rears up large and ripples against death's certain pressures, generating mesmerizing suspense and surprising empathy. Yielding poignant insights into the nature of love and loss, savagery and splendor, *Being Dead* asserts itself as a new American gothic—hugely powerful, majestically unassuming, and keenly unsettling.

A tragic accident, shrouded in mystery, leads to a family reunion in the hidden village of Little Hatchet, located in the smothering shadow of GodBeGone Wood, the home of the mythical Woodcutter and Grandma. Alec Eades rediscovers his bond with GodBeGone Wood and the future his father agreed to years ago as nefarious landowner Oliver Hayward schemes to raise money for the village by re-enacting part of the Woodcutter legend. Old wounds are reopened and ties of blood and friendship are tested to the extreme when the Woodcutter is summoned and Grandma returns.

According to Dante, a **sin** is the misdirection of love-the human will, or essentially, the direction of our beings. Love the Sinner is an examination of just how those sins can kaleidoscope into **horrific** consequences creating a distorted and **deadly** landscape. These stories stand stark before you in full glaring misstep and **macabre** to show the human psyche in all its twisted reality. From grief and its rage to medical meddling to ensure a new world order to bloody **revenge** within a quantum leap, these stories seek to solidify one absolute truth: man is the scariest **monster**.

Visit our website at: www.brigidsgatepress.co